THE TAMING OF LADY LORINDA

As Lorinda selected her evening gown, she carefully mapped her strategy.

If she was to gain her own way and enslave her willful young husband as she had all her other admirers, she must first captivate him. She would force herself to be charming, even though she told herself that she hated him vehemently.

"He shall love me," she said grimly, "and when he does, I shall scorn him as I have all the others."

BARBARA CARTLAND

Bantam Books by Barbara Cartland
Ask your bookseller for the books you have missed

1 THE DARING DECEPTION
2 NO DARKNESS FOR LOVE
3 THE LITTLE ADVENTURE
4 LESSONS IN LOVE
5 JOURNEY TO PARADISE
6 THE BORED BRIDEGROOM
7 THE PENNILESS PEER
8 THE DANGEROUS DANDY
9 THE RUTHLESS RAKE
10 THE WICKED MARQUIS
11 THE CASTLE OF FEAR
12 THE GLITTERING LIGHTS
13 A SWORD TO THE HEART
14 THE KARMA OF LOVE
15 THE MAGNIFICENT
    MARRIAGE
16 BEWITCHED
17 THE IMPETUOUS
    DUCHESS
18 THE FRIGHTENED BRIDE
19 THE SHADOW OF SIN
20 THE FLAME IS LOVE
21 THE TEARS OF LOVE
22 A VERY NAUGHTY ANGEL
23 CALL OF THE HEART
24 THE DEVIL IN LOVE
25 AS EAGLES FLY
26 LOVE IS INNOCENT
27 SAY YES, SAMANTHA
28 THE CRUEL COUNT
29 THE MASK OF LOVE

30 FIRE ON THE SNOW
31 AN ARROW OF LOVE
32 A GAMBLE WITH HEARTS
33 A KISS FOR THE KING
34 A FRAME OF DREAMS
35 THE FRAGRANT FLOWER
36 THE ELUSIVE EARL
37 MOON OVER EDEN
38 THE GOLDEN ILLUSION
39 THE HUSBAND HUNTERS
40 NO TIME FOR LOVE
41 PASSIONS IN THE SAND
42 THE SLAVES OF LOVE
43 AN ANGEL IN HELL
44 THE WILD CRY OF LOVE
45 THE BLUE-EYED WITCH
46 THE INCREDIBLE
    HONEYMOON
47 A DREAM FROM THE
    NIGHT
48 CONQUERED BY LOVE
49 NEVER LAUGH AT LOVE
50 THE SECRET OF THE
    GLEN
51 THE PROUD PRINCESS
52 HUNGRY FOR LOVE
53 THE HEART TRIUMPHANT
54 THE DREAM AND
    THE GLORY
55 THE TAMING OF
    LADY LORINDA

Barbara Cartland

The Taming of Lady Lorinda

BANTAM BOOKS · TORONTO · NEW YORK · LONDON

THE TAMING OF LADY LORINDA
A Bantam Book | January 1977

ISBN 0–553–10339–3

Published simultaneously in the United States and Canada

Bantam Books are published by Bantam Books, Inc. Its trade-
mark, consisting of the words "Bantam Books" and the por-
trayal of a bantam, is registered in the United States Patent
Office and in other countries. Marca Registrada. Bantam
Books, Inc., 666 Fifth Avenue, New York, New York 10019.

The Taming
of Lady Lorinda

CHAPTER ONE

1794

The Man in the Green Mask stood looking down into the Ball-Room.

It was a kaleidoscope of colour and glitter under the crystal chandeliers.

The guests had been invited to "Come as your Fancy," and there were inevitably a dozen Cleopatras, a large number of Jesters, and a predominance of Elizabethan head-dresses and ruffs.

As he stared at the couples dancing to the music of a Band in the Minstrels' Gallery, the Man in the Green Mask stiffened as he said with a surprised note in his voice to the friend standing beside him:

"I thought you were bringing me to a Ball where I would meet the *Beau Monde*."

"That is where you are."

"And these are not pretty Cyprians?"

"Certainly not! They are the *Ton* of Society, Ladies of Quality who grace the noblest families in the land."

"I can hardly believe it!"

As the Man in the Green Mask spoke, he stared not at the pouting red lips which showed below the velvet masks, nor at the eyes which glittered through them,

1

nor at the rounded columns of bejewelled white
throats.

Instead he looked at the pink-tipped breasts showing through the transparent draperies, which seemed to
reveal rather than conceal the curves of the slim hips
and the exquisitely sculptured legs, which in most
cases were naked.

"Am I really in England?" he ejaculated at last.

His friend laughed.

"You have been away too long. There have been
many changes and, as you will learn, most of them not
for the better."

"When I went abroad," the Man in the Green Mask
said, "women were respectable and subservient, gentle, and obedient to their husbands."

"That is completely out-of-date," his informant told
him. "Today women are not weaklings, they go in for
horse and carriage races, they join shooting parties,
they play cricket against other teams of women, and
in the case of the Royal Princesses, football as well!"

"Good God!"

"They consider themselves to be the equal of the
male, and this shows itself in their appearance."

"I noticed that powder has disappeared."

"Both for the women and for the men, thank God!
Of course we can thank the Prince of Wales for the
vogue of *au naturel*."

"It is certainly a relief as far as we are concerned,"
the Man in the Green Mask remarked, "but for women
it is a different matter."

"The new order," his friend said with laughter in his
voice, "demands '*la victim coiffure*,' which of course is
the revolutionary influence from France."

He made a gesture with his hand as he explained:

"Gone are the high, elaborate creations of the old
regime. Now we have wind-swept locks carefully tou-
sled and, to complete the illusion, a thin strap of crimson velvet to encircle the neck."

"I should have thought, considering the sufferings at
the guillotine, that is in extremely bad taste!" the
Man in the Green Mask remarked.

"My dear fellow, a lot of things we do are in bad taste, but we all continue to do them."

He glanced at his companion with a mischievous expression before he went on:

"Many of the gowns worn at Carlton House leave the breasts actually uncovered, or draped with such a fine material that there is nothing left to the imagination."

The Man in the Green Mask did not reply.

He only continued to watch the dancers on the floor a little below them, noting that the dance itself was becoming wilder and the movements of the participants more exaggerated.

"You may think me old-fashioned—" he began, then his voice died away to silence.

The long French windows leading into the garden were open since it was a hot June evening, and now through them there entered unexpectedly and surprisingly a black horse.

Riding it was a woman who appeared at first glance to be completely naked, except for her long, red-gold hair, which reached below her waist.

It was only on closer inspection that an observer was able to notice that her saddle, which was Mexican in shape and ornamented in silver, was high at the front and at the back.

Also that her hair was arranged so that all that could really be seen of her body was her naked arms and legs.

She was however riding astride, which in itself was daring, and as if she disdained a disguise, she was not wearing a mask. Her large green eyes, which seemed to fill her whole face, were alight with amusement.

The Man in the Green Mask found his voice.

"Good God! Who is that?"

"That," his companion replied, "is Lady Lorinda Camborne, the greatest hoyden of them all."

"Can she really come from a reputable family?"

"Her father is the Earl of Camborne and Cardis."

"If he had any sense, he would give his daughter a good beating, and take her home."

"He is unlikely to see her, since he never raises his eyes from the card-table!"

"He is a gambler?"

"Compulsive!"

"This girl—how old is she?"

"Lady Lorinda is twenty, I think. She has certainly to my knowledge been the toast of St. James's for two years."

"She is really admired?"

"You are being too censorious! She may behave in a somewhat reprehensible manner, and I am not denying that her escapades keep the gossips in a continual twitter; but at least she is exceptionally, even soul-destroyingly beautiful."

The Man in the Green Mask did not speak. He was watching Lady Lorinda ride her black stallion, a magnificent animal, round the Ball-Room.

The dancers had stopped to applaud her, with all the men shouting encouragement, some of them throwing flowers at her as she passed.

"The betting at White's was that she would not appear naked," the Man in the Green Mask was informed. "Well, she has not only won her bet, but a great deal of money will change hands, as it has after every other outrageous prank in which she has taken part."

Having circled the Ball-Room twice, Lady Lorinda acknowledged the plaudits of the crowd and then, as unexpectedly as she had arrived, disappeared through the window into the garden.

"Is that the last we shall see of her?" the Man in the Green Mask asked.

"Heavens, no! Her Ladyship will return, arrayed in some other flight of fancy—and certainly nothing which will make her anonymous! She will be one of the last to leave."

"She enjoys this sort of festivity?"

There was something scornful in the question.

"Apparently. It is the way she spends her life— parties every night, wild excursions to Vauxhall or to less savoury night-haunts. And wherever she goes she leaves behind a trail of broken hearts."

There was a pause before the speaker continued:

"There are many stories about Lady Lorinda—the latest is that the Marquis of Queensbury . . ."

"Good Lord, is that old goat still about?" the Man in the Green Mask interposed.

"Only death will put an end to his lechery! As I was saying, he fancied himself in the role of Paris judging who should receive the golden apple inscribed 'for the fairest.'"

"Three goddesses all claimed it—if I remember the story right."

"You are correct."

"And they were naked?"

"Of course!"

"One of them being Lady Lorinda?"

"So I am told."

"And men actually fall in love with a woman like that?"

"Of course they do! And I will say one thing for Lady Lorinda: she has courage and personality, which is often sadly lacking in her contemporaries. No-one can ignore her."

"Or fail to notice her!" the Man in the Green Mask said dryly.

"I think I must introduce you to her," said his companion, smiling. "It will do Her Ladyship good to meet a man who is not knocked flat by her beauty and does not allow himself to be trampled under her pretty feet."

He paused before he added:

"In the meantime I see the Prince of Wales has arrived. Come—let me present you. I know he will be delighted to hear from you the news from another part of the world."

Later in the evening the Man in the Green Mask left the Supper-Room, where he had eaten at the Royal Table, and finding it extremely hot in the Ball-Room he walked into the garden.

The dance was being given at Hampstead and it was like, the Man in the Green Mask thought, being in the country.

There was just a faint breeze stirring the branches of the huge trees, from the flower-beds came the fragrance of night-scented stock, and the stars were brilliant in the sky above.

He drew in a deep breath, thinking as he did so how different the air seemed from the suffocating heat of India.

As he stood alone he suddenly heard a man's voice say:

"For God's sake, Lorinda, listen to me. I love you! Marry me, or I swear I will kill myself!"

The Man in the Green Mask stiffened.

There was an anguish in the voice that was unmistakable.

"Marry me, Lorinda, and make me the happiest man alive."

"Is this the tenth or the eleventh time, Edward, that I have refused you?"

The Man in the Green Mask realised that the two people speaking were just on the other side of a high yew-hedge.

It was impossible in the darkness for him to see through it, but he fancied they were sitting on a seat with their backs to the hedge, and he was actually only a few feet away from them.

"I have asked you before and I ask you again—marry me!"

"And every time I refuse. Really, Edward, you are becoming a monumental bore! I would like to go back to the Ball-Room."

"Do not leave, Lorinda. Please stay with me. I will not bore you. I will do anything you want—anything! —if only you will care for me a little."

"Why should I? If I wanted a lap-dog I would buy one."

The voice was scornful. Then quickly came the words:

"If you touch me I swear I will never speak to you again."

"Lorinda! Lorinda!"

The cry was desperate. Then there was the sound of a woman's heels moving away along a flagged path and the anguished groan of the man left behind.

The Man in the Green Mask realised that the conversation to which he had been listening was over.

Now he too retraced his steps to the Ball-Room.

It was not difficult to identify Lady Lorinda, and the moment he stepped through the French window he heard her voice, gay and unconcerned by what had just passed.

She was wearing with great daring the embroidered full-skirted coat of a Cavalier.

The long satin breeches, be-ribboned over their silk stockings and revealing her slim ankles, were certainly outrageous. Her red-gold hair had been curled and arranged like a periwig beneath a feathered hat.

She wore a mask, but it did not conceal her small straight nose, her perfectly curved lips, or the proud manner in which she carried her pointed chin.

She had a glass of wine in her hand and as the Man in the Green Mask entered the Ball-Room she and those round her were drinking to the health of their host, a dark, rather sardonic-looking man of middle age.

He acknowledged those who toasted him, but his eyes were on Lady Lorinda and when the toast was drunk he went to her side.

"Let me take you into the garden. I want to talk to you."

They were standing near to the Man in the Green Mask, who could overhear what they said.

"I have just come from the garden," Lady Lorinda said, pouting. "If you are thinking of making love to me, Ulric, then let me warn you that I am in no mood for it."

"Why should you suspect that was my intention?"

"Because love is all men ever talk about," she retorted. "Is there no other topic of conversation?"

"Not when they are talking to you!"

"Love bores me! It is a subject about which I have no interest, and therefore if you wish to amuse me you must talk of something else."

"Are you still pretending you have no heart?"

"I am not pretending, I am just fortunate! Let us go to the Supper-Room. I am beginning to fancy that I am hungry."

They moved away and the Man in the Green Mask stood looking after them.

"I told you she was beautiful, but unpredictable," a voice said beside him, and he saw his friend with whom he had arrived at the Ball.

"Does everyone fall at her feet and do as she tells them?" the Man in the Green Mask asked.

"Everyone obeys Lady Lorinda."

"And if they do not?"

"She ceases to count them among her acquaintances. Such ostracism, I am told, is worse than being excommunicated!"

The Man in the Green Mask laughed.

"I have a feeling that since I have been away you have all lost a sense of values, or should I say a sense of humour?"

Much later in the evening when the guests had begun to thin out and the first faint light of dawn was beginning to sweep away the stars in the sky, the two friends drove through the drive-gates and onto the high road.

They were in a Phaeton, with only a groom up behind, and the horses were of exceptionally fine quality.

"You enjoyed yourself?" the driver of the team enquired.

His friend, who no longer wore a mask, laughed.

"It was certainly a revelation! I expected to find changes, but not to the extent I have seen tonight."

"Are you thinking of the men or the women?"

"The Prince surprised me, for one. He has grown fat, and I was certainly not impressed by his boon companions."

"Who would be?" the driver of the horses asked.
"And now tell me what you think of the women. Are
you very shocked?"

The Man who had worn the Green Mask laughed.

"I assure you that nothing shocks me. But I am certainly appalled to think that these indecent, irrespon-
sible creatures will be the mothers of the next generation."

"Are you thinking of doing anything about it?"

"What do you suggest I do?"

"Reform Lady Lorinda! What a challenge that would
be for any man!"

"It should be possible."

"Who has ever tamed a tigress? I will wager you any
sum you would like to mention that it is a complete
and absolute impossibility."

The Man who had worn the Green Mask was silent
before he said slowly:

"One thousand guineas!"

"Are you serious?"

His friend's voice was incredulous. Then he laughed.

"I will take you! I would not miss the outcome of
this Herculean task for ten times the sum."

They had driven on a short distance when he suddenly exclaimed:

"Talk of a tigress—in female form! There she is just
ahead of us!"

He pointed to where moving up the hill towards
Spaniards Inn there was a black travelling-chariot, the
panels of the doors embellished with the Camborne
coat-of-arms.

It would not have been particularly noticeable except for the livery of the coachmen and the footmen
standing up behind.

Instead of the ordinary colours prevalent amongst
the aristocracy such as blue, green, or claret, Lady Lorinda's retainers were in white trimmed with silver.

The Man who had worn the Green Mask stared at it
in his astonishment.

The chariot reached the summit of the hill, then

having passed through the narrow opening between the Spaniards Inn and the toll-gate it came to a sudden halt.

"What is happening?" the driver of the Phaeton enquired, then gave an exclamation: "Good God, Footpads! Her Ladyship is being held up!"

He whipped his horses forward, but as he did so there was a sudden loud report of a pistol-shot and they saw the man who had been standing at the open door of the chariot fall backwards onto the side of the road. The other man who was with him ran away.

Before they could draw up behind the chariot the footman standing behind, who had his hands up, was jerked forward and the vehicle moved on.

The Phaeton stopped beside the Footpad.

He lay sprawling in the ditch, his arms flung wide, one hand still holding a pistol.

He was masked and looked an extremely unprepossessing type of felon. There was no mistaking the crimson patch of blood spreading over his chest.

The groom had jumped down from the back of the Phaeton.

"He's quite dead, M'Lord," he announced.

The driver touched his horses with the whip.

"In which case it is none of our business," he replied and drove on.

There was silence for a little while. Then the Man who had worn the Green Mask said:

"Was there someone with the girl or did she shoot that man herself?"

"Of course she shot him!" his friend replied. "And it is not the first time!"

There was amusement in his voice as he continued:

"Here you have seen a perfect example of how the young women of today can look after themselves. I have been told of the way Lady Lorinda deals with Footpads and Highwaymen. Now I have seen her in action!"

He laughed before he continued:

"Apparently as soon as a robber opens the door she

shoots to kill. Her servants do not even have the trouble of protecting her."

"I am astonished!" his companion remarked. "In my day, women burst into frightened sobs and expected a manly arm to protect them."

"There are still some of the clinging type, if that is what you prefer, and with your wealth they will cling all the closer!"

There was no answer and they drove on over Hampstead Heath in silence.

* * *

Lady Lorinda was in fact lying back in her carriage with closed eyes.

She had however taken the precaution of reloading the pistol she held in her lap before she allowed herself to relax.

Hampstead Heath was notorious for Footpads and she disliked them as much, she thought, as she disliked the would-be lovers who pestered her however brutally she rid herself of their plaintive pleadings.

Lord Edward Hinton was only one of her many admirers who would not take no for an answer.

Thinking over how tiresome he had been the whole evening, she decided that in the future she would make it clear that if Edward was going to be in a party she would refuse the invitation.

Nothing she could say or do stopped him from pleading with her to be his wife and making in her own words "a damned nuisance of himself."

Their host, Lord Wroxford, was not much better, but at least while he pursued her he could not offer marriage.

He was already married and his proposition was therefore strictly dishonourable, and as such, Lorinda thought, easier to deal with.

She could laugh Ulric to scorn and they both knew that she was no more likely to give in to his suggestions than she was to jump over the moon.

Ulric nevertheless went on trying, wittily, cynically, and amusingly, but Edward was different.

He had threatened so often to kill himself if she

would not marry him that Lorinda was bored even before he opened his mouth to speak.

Yet Edward would in fact make her a very suitable husband, and there was always the possibility that if his elder brother continued to father daughters and no male heir, he would someday be a Duke.

"If I were sensible I would accept him," Lorinda told herself, "but how could I tolerate his whining after me for the rest of my life?"

She felt in the same way about so many men, and many of them not only had so much wealth to offer her but also an established place in Society.

Only Lorinda realised how precarious her hold was over the fickle pleasure-seeking crowd who were equally prepared to cheer or boo as the spirit moved them.

"What do I want?" Lorinda asked herself now as the carriage descended Hampstead Hill and there was no longer any danger.

She had a sudden vision of Balls and parties going on interminably, of the same raffish set with which she was so familiar travelling with her from London to Brighton, to Newmarket for the races, to Bath to take the waters, and back to London for another round of frenzied gaiety.

Was that what she really wanted or desired of life?

She was well aware that tomorrow all the Dowagers who disapproved of her would be chattering together like the parrots in the Zoo over her appearance as Lady Godiva.

Lord Barrymore, a dissolute Peer, had wagered that she would not dare do it, and that was all the incentive Lorinda ever needed to be outrageous.

"I can do anything I like," she said aloud.

She laughed to think how the story of her behaviour, which would lose nothing in the telling, would be carried by the gossips to the King and Queen at Windsor Castle.

They would undoubtedly attribute it to the pernicious and debauched example set by the Prince of Wales.

"Sanctimonious old humbugs!" Lorinda exclaimed.

She saw with relief that the journey had ended and the chariot was drawing up outside Camborne House in Hanover Square.

It was a large, uncomfortable, rather ugly Mansion which had been built by the seventh Earl of Camborne, who had been Lorinda's grandfather.

She had done her best to brighten it with innovations of her own.

She thought as the footman opened the door wearing the white and silver livery which she had designed that it was certainly less gloomy than it had been when she was a child.

"Is His Lordship in, Thomas?" she enquired.

"Yes, M'Lady. His Lordship came home half an hour ago and is in the Library."

"Thank you, Thomas."

Lorinda threw her cloak onto a chair and did not realise that the footman was looking at her masculine attire with horrified eyes as she walked over the marble floor towards the Library.

She opened the door.

Her father was sitting at his desk in the centre of the room and he was loading a duelling-pistol.

The Earl of Camborne and Cardis looked up in surprise at his daughter's entrance.

He was a handsome man with greying hair and the sallow complexion of one who did not obtain enough fresh air. The gaming-rooms were notoriously stuffy.

He put down the pistol he was holding rather too quickly for it to be a natural movement, as he exclaimed:

"I was not expecting you back so early, Lorinda."

"What has happened, Papa? Do not tell me you are about to fight a duel?"

Her father did not answer and she walked towards the desk to stand looking down at him.

"Tell me, Papa."

It seemed as if the Earl was about to refuse to do as she asked. Then he flung himself back in his chair to say defiantly:

"I was intending to shoot myself!"

"Papa, you cannot be serious!"

"I have lost everything we possess."

For a moment Lorinda was still. Then she sat down on the chair opposite to him.

"Tell me exactly what has happened."

"I was playing with Charles Fox," the Earl replied.

Lorinda's lips tightened.

She knew only too well that Charles James Fox was the most dangerous opponent her father could have chosen.

A Whig Politician of amazing eloquence, Charles Fox, paunchy, untidy, graceless, with a double chin and black shaggy eye-brows, was a man of extraordinary charm.

Detested by the King, he had in consequence become a close friend of the Prince of Wales. In fact at one time the Prince's regard for him had been near to idolatry.

The son of an enormously rich man, Charles Fox had developed an insatiable passion for gambling at Eton, and when he was only sixteen he and his brother lost thirty-two thousand pounds in one evening!

It was ironic, Lorinda thought, that on one of the few occasions that Charles Fox was the winner at gambling it should be at the expense of her father.

His next words confirmed what she already feared.

"I was winning, Lorinda," the Earl said in a tired voice, "winning quite a considerable sum, when Fox's luck changed. I thought it could not last, but when I rose from the tables I had nothing else left to stake."

There was a pause before Lorinda asked in a quite steady voice:

"How much have you lost?"

"One hundred thousand pounds!"

It was not an astronomical sum of money to many of those who gambled at White's Club, but Lorinda knew as well as her father did that to them it meant disaster.

They had their house in London and the family home in Cornwall but only a comparatively small income and, while they appeared to be opulent and lived in an extravagant manner, it was simply and solely because they always optimistically believed that "something would turn up."

This meant that when the Earl had a good run at the tables Lorinda took his winnings from him before he could lose them again.

But never before had his losses approached anything like a hundred thousand pounds.

"There is only one thing for me to do," the Earl said hoarsely, "and that is to shoot myself. Fox can hardly expect me to settle the debt if I am no longer in this world."

"You know as well as I do, Papa," Lorinda replied, "that it is a debt of honour and that somehow I should have to pay it."

"Do you mean that?"

"Of course I mean it," she replied, "and all I can say is that if you intend to leave me alone to pick up the pieces it is a very shabby trick!"

She spoke scornfully. Then she rose to her feet to walk to the window and pull back the heavy velvet curtains.

Now the dawn had broken and the first faint fingers of gold showed above the roof-tops.

"I thought," the Earl said behind her in an uncertain voice, "that if I were dead Fox would cancel the debt and it would be an easy way out."

"Easy for you, but not for me," Lorinda said quietly, "and whatever else the Cambornes may have been, they were certainly not cowards!"

"Damnit, I will not have you calling me a coward," her father said sharply.

"I cannot imagine anything more cowardly than for you to walk out on me," she answered.

Her father pushed his pistol to one side impatiently.

"If that is your attitude, you might like to think of a solution."

"It is obvious, is it not?" she asked, turning round from the window to move back to the desk.

"I see nothing obvious about it."

"Very well then, I will tell you," she answered. "We

shall have to sell this house and the contents of it.
That should fetch quite a considerable sum, and we
will then retire to Cornwall."

"To Cornwall?"

"Why not?—until we sell the Priory, if anyone
would give us anything for it."

The Earl brought his fist down with such force that
the ink-pot rattled.

"I will not sell the home of my forebears since before the Norman Conquest!" he shouted. "Although it
is not entailed, no Camborne has ever sunk so low as
to sell the birthplace of his ancestors."

Lorinda shrugged her shoulders.

"You may have to," she replied. "I doubt if this
house and everything it contains, including Mama's
jewellery, will fetch even fifty thousand pounds!"

The Earl put his hands up to his face.

"Oh—God!" he ejaculated. "Why the devil was I
such a fool?"

"Regrets will get you nowhere," Lorinda said coldly.
"We have to be practical about this, Papa, and I presume that means that I shall have to see to everything. You must ask Charles Fox for time to pay. You
will certainly not be able to give him a hundred thousand pounds within the usual two weeks."

"Have I to go on my knees to him as well as
suffer every other humiliation?" the Earl asked
angrily.

"It is your debt," Lorinda said.

He looked up at her and saw an expression in her
green eyes which made him exclaim furiously:

"God Almighty! You might be a little more sym-
pathetic and understanding! Have you no feeling for
me or for anyone else?"

"If you want to know the truth," Lorinda said, "I
despise you."

She paused and her father did not speak as she went
on:

"I despise you as I despise all men. You are all the
same, weak as water when it comes to your own de-
sires. Yet you expect a woman to croon over your stu-

pidity and weep over your misdemeanours. Well, let me make it quite clear, I shall do neither!"

She picked up the pistol from the desk and said sharply:

"I will take this with me in case you cannot be trusted with it. Tomorrow I will start to sell the only place I know of as home and see if I can get a fancy price for the treasures our ancestors collected and the jewellery which gave my mother so much pleasure."

She walked towards the door, then turned back to look at her father, the light from the candles glittering on her red hair.

"If it upsets you too much," she said contemptuously, "I suggest you leave immediately for Cornwall and start putting into some semblance of order the ruins that are left us there."

* * *

The following morning Lorinda awoke from a deep sleep and as her maid pulled back the curtains she remembered the task that lay ahead of her.

She did not feel panic-stricken, as any other young girl might have felt, at the magnitude of the difficulties that confronted her, or, as she well knew, the inadequacy of her father to cope with any of it.

Her mother had died when Lorinda was twelve.

While she remembered her with affection, she had always felt she had little in common with the soft, gentle person who had thought her father wonderful and was prepared to accept his precarious mode of living without doing anything to alter it.

Lorinda was a throw-back to her Camborne ancestors who had fought in the great battles of Cornishmen against innumerable enemies.

Cornwall had been the last portion of Britain in the south to submit to the Saxon invaders, and the Cambornes had fought against King Egbert and refused to acknowledge his supremacy.

Ninety years later they had helped Aethelstan to drive back the West Welsh from Exeter and make the Tamar the boundary of their territory.

All down the ages the Cambornes had been fiercely

independent: they had fought in support of the Lancastrian cause and been prominent among the troops led by Sir Bevil Grenville when he defeated the Parliamentarians at Bradock.

There was a fire in Lorinda's veins which did not seem to have survived in her father's.

She would not submit to domination, and she had always revolted against authority since she had been a small child.

"You twist and turn yourself out of doing what you are told like the Cornish wrestlers who fought at Agincourt," her Nurse said to her when she was tiny.

And she was still twisting and turning, in this moment of adversity against accepting the inevitable, as her father was evidently prepared to do.

Lorinda was silent as she let her maid help her to dress and arrange her hair in the fashionable windswept curls that seemed to have been especially designed to show her small heart-shaped face at its best.

She was not small, in fact she was taller than the average woman.

But she was so slim and graceful that men instinctively wished to protect her, only to find her will of iron and her unconquerable pride at variance with her exceptional feminine beauty.

That she was beautiful could not be denied, and yet as Lorinda looked in the mirror she wondered if her beauty had brought her any happiness.

She was well aware that if she asked the advice of any of the Society hostesses who had chaperoned her so often at her father's request since she emerged on London Society, their advice would all be the same:

"Marry a rich man."

She could almost hear them saying it, knowing that it would be all too easy for her to accept Edward Hinton, Anthony Dawlish, Chistopher Conway, or any of the other young aristocrats who had laid their hearts at her feet.

They would doubtless, she thought as she finished dressing, be only too eager to come running to the house should she send them a note demanding their attendance.

But something proud and part of her heritage made her feel disgust at the thought of accepting a husband merely because it was expedient.

She walked downstairs with her head held high, her brain busy planning, manoeuvring, almost as if she were a man going into battle rather than a woman who should have no knowledge of such tactics.

She entered the Library to find that her father had not been to bed.

He was asleep in the high wing-back armchair at the side of the fireplace, and an empty decanter beside him told its own story.

She shook him sharply by the shoulder.

"Wake up, Papa!"

She had realised when she spoke to him last night that he had had a lot to drink, but the amount he had consumed after she had left him had made his eyes bloodshot and he smelt of spirits.

"Wake up, Papa!" she said again, and now the Earl opened his eyes.

"Oh, it is you, Lorinda! What do you want?"

"I want you to wash and get dressed," she answered. "It is morning, and there is breakfast on the table if you require it."

The Earl shuddered.

"Give me a drink!"

Lorinda did not argue with him. She went to the grog-tray which stood in a corner of the Library and poured him out a stiff brandy, holding the glass out to him disdainfully.

He took it from her and gulped it down.

"What is the time?"

"Nine o'clock. Are you going to Cornwall, or are you staying here with me? I warn you it will not be very comfortable. I intend to dismiss the servants as soon as we have had breakfast."

Fortified by the brandy, the Earl rose to his feet.

A servant had obviously been in to pull back the

curtains, and the sun was streaming in through the windows, one of which was opened onto the small courtyard at the back of the house.

The beds were bright with flowers and Lorinda found herself thinking how much it had cost to have them potted out and arranged there by a gardener who came to tend them four times a week.

"There is—something I did not tell you last night," the Earl said after a moment.

"What is that?"

"You prevented me from doing the honourable thing, as I intended to do," he said, "so you may as well know the truth."

"The truth?" Lorinda asked sharply.

"I was seen cheating towards the end of the game!"

"Cheating?"

It was a cry rather than an exclamation.

"I was drunk and desperate—I was not even very skilful at it."

"How many people know?"

"Fox, and three other members of White's who were at the table. They are all friends of mine and I think they will keep quiet, but I would not dare to enter the Club again for some months."

This was a blow that Lorinda had not expected.

She was well aware that a man who was caught cheating was a social outcast, a pariah to his fellow men.

There was a chance, just a chance, since her father was exceedingly popular, that those who had seen what had happened would pretend it was an accident due to drunkenness and would say nothing about it.

But she knew that her father was right when he said he should not go back to White's.

For a moment she almost regretted that she had not allowed him to do as he had intended and take his life.

It was in fact considered to be the only honourable action open to a man who had behaved in such a manner.

Then she told herself that that would have been even more cowardly.

"There is nothing you can do, Papa," she said in a quite steady, normal voice, "but to leave immediately for Cornwall. Take one of the grooms with you, whichever you wish to keep, and two of the best horses. The rest will be sold."

Her voice was quite impersonal as she continued:

"I will bring all your personal belongings down with me in the travelling-carriage."

"What about my Phaeton?"

"As it is newer than the rest of our vehicles it will fetch the most money and must be left behind. I am now going to have breakfast, then I shall be talking to the staff. If you want me I will be in the Morning-Room."

She moved towards the door. As she reached it her father said in a low voice:

"I am sorry, Lorinda."

She walked from the room without looking back.

CHAPTER TWO

Lorinda looked at the empty hall-table with a wry smile.

It seemed incredible that only a week ago it had been covered with visiting-cards, loaded down with invitations, and usually supporting innumerable bouquets of flowers left by her ardent admirers.

She thought that if anything could make her detest men more than she did already, it was what had happened once the whisper had gone round London that the Earl of Camborne and Cardis was selling up.

Lorinda told herself she had expected what had occurred, but even so it had been a shock.

The day after the party at Hampstead Heath she had received the usual number of adulatory notes, a profusion of flowers, and the knocker on the door at Hanover Square was never still.

Her father was not in a fit state to travel, but she forced him to write a letter to Charles Fox telling him that the debt would be paid as quickly as possible and that the proceeds of the Sale would be forwarded to him by the firm which had been engaged to conduct it.

"He will be lucky if he ever gets the rest!" the Earl had growled as he finished writing.

"I cannot allow you to be a defaulter, Papa," Lorinda replied. "We will find the money somehow, even if it takes us a life-time."

The Earl muttered an oath under his breath and poured himself another drink.

It was two days later before he set off for Cornwall, taking with him two of his best horses and the most reliable of the grooms he employed.

Lorinda thought that even such a small concession was in some degree cheating the man to whom they owed so much money, but she made no protest aloud.

She only thought as her father rode away that it was typical that he never even enquired as to how she would manage without him.

Actually she was quite sure he would be more of a nuisance than a help, but the task of selling the house and packing what they must take with them seemed extremely formidable.

Two of the older servants who had been with them a long time had agreed to help Lorinda until she too left the house.

The rest had all been dismissed and she sat down to write them glowing references so that they would have no difficulty in finding other employment.

The firm she had engaged to conduct the Sale was, she was thankful to learn, fairly optimistic that a considerable sum of money could be raised.

She had feared that the house, being so large, might prove to be a "white elephant," but almost immediately the Estate Agents began to send people to view it.

Although Lorinda had the suspicion that it would not continue to be a private residence but would be given over to gaming, she was not prepared to argue.

A few of the pictures were valuable and the furniture which had not been knocked about over the ages was salable. But they had never been able to afford to replace the worn carpets or many of the threadbare curtains, and these, she knew, would fetch nothing.

If she had been inclined to brood or feel depressed about what was taking place round her, she certainly had little time in which to do so.

Every moment of the day, one or another of the servants was asking her what was to be packed and what was to be left behind, and the men who were taking an inventory of what was to be sold and numbering furniture always seemed to be in the way.

One thing which had unaccountably hurt Lorinda, although she would not acknowledge it even to herself, was the behaviour of Lord Edward Hinton.

Despite the fact that she had always treated him so harshly, she had in her extremity remembered his protestations of love and thought that at least he would be loyal, whoever else ignored her plight.

But two days after the party at Hampstead she had received a note from him which read:

Lorinda,

Owing to circumstances over which I have no control, I am obliged to leave London. You know full well what my feelings have been for you this past year and, although you have made it very clear that I mean nothing to you, I could not go without saying good-bye.

Good-bye, beautiful, green-eyed Lorinda. I shall always remember you.

Edward

She stared for a long time at what had been written. Then she went in search of her father, who had not yet left for Cornwall.

"Tell me, Papa," she asked, "who were your friends at White's who were present when you lost so much money to Charles Fox and most unfortunately saw you cheating?"

She saw by her father's face that he resented the question, but she stood waiting for his answer. After a moment he said sulkily:

"Davenport and Charles Lambeth were there."

"And the Duke of Dorset?" Lorinda asked.

Her father nodded.

She walked away without saying any more.

Now she knew the explanation for Edward's note.

The Duke and Duchess of Dorset had always disapproved of her and she was well aware that she was the last person they desired as a daughter-in-law.

The Duke was very strait-laced and more than anything else he would resent and avoid being connected in any way with a card-cheat.

Edward was completely dependent upon his father and the Duke must have acted swiftly.

She was sure without his saying it that Edward would either be sent abroad or be forced to spend his time at the Duke's country seat until the danger was past.

"Why should I expect anyone to stand by me?" she asked.

At the same time, she had never felt more alone or isolated.

When there was no-one at the door except the tradesmen, she quoted to herself with a cynical smile: "The higher they rise the harder they fall!"

She heard the rat-tat of the knocker at that moment and thought that it would be one of the men who were preparing the house for tomorrow's Sale.

The maids were upstairs packing the last of the possessions which she intended to take with her to Cornwall, so she opened the door.

Standing outside, looking more sardonic than usual, was Lord Wroxford.

Lorinda looked at him for a moment, then said:

"I am not at home, Ulric."

"I want to speak to you, Lorinda," he replied. "May I come in?"

She hesitated, then with a gesture opened the door wide.

"Have you come to spy out the land?" she asked. "Or did you want to reserve some special object which has taken your fancy?"

There was a mocking note in her voice. Lorinda was well aware that Lord Wroxford's house in Hampstead was filled with treasures and nothing her father possessed was likely to be of interest to him.

"I want to talk to you," he replied, putting his hat down on a table.

"I will try to find you a chair on which to sit," Lorinda answered, "but they are all stacked ready for the Auctioneer."

She led the way into the Library, which looked particularly depressing with empty shelves from which the books had been removed.

The carpets had been rolled up, the chairs corded together, and the pictures propped against the wall.

Lord Wroxford, however, looked only at Lorinda, thinking she was even more beautiful than usual, her hair fiery red against the whiteness of her skin.

She stood still in the centre of the room.

"Well, what have you to say?" she asked in an uncompromising tone.

"I have come to suggest that I take you away from all this unpleasantness."

Lorinda gave him a sharp glance, but she did not speak and he went on:

"We can go abroad, out of sight of all the malicious gossips. I am convinced, as I have always been, that we would deal well together."

Lorinda smiled.

"It is kind of you to ask me, Ulric, but I think you know my answer."

"What have you to lose?" he asked. "Only this mess into which your father has dragged you."

Lorinda put her head a little to one side.

"I wonder how long it would be before I bored you?" she asked. "I think you are not the type, Ulric, who would find the world well lost for love."

"If you loved me," he answered, "I confidently believe that I would never have any regrets or ever wish to see England again."

"If!" she exclaimed. "That is the operative word! You know as well as I do that I would be bored with you almost before we started."

"I want you, Lorinda! I could teach you to love me."

Lorinda laughed.

"Are you really fool enough to believe that? I dislike all men and I shall never love one! Love is a condition of which I have no knowledge and in which I have no interest."

He took a step towards her.

"Dammit, Lorinda! You are enough to try the patience of a saint!"

"And you are no saint!"

She looked at him with her eyes full of mischief as she said:

"I know only too well, Ulric, how you have keyed yourself up into making this proposition, hoping at the back of your mind that I would not accept it."

"That is not true!" he contradicted. "You excite me to madness—you always have! If you have any sense you will come away with me and let me protect you."

"I never did have any sense," Lorinda replied, "and I know so much better than you do that we would be quarrelling before we had even crossed the Channel. You would want to touch me, and I loathe being touched!"

She spoke with a vehemence which struck away the fire that had been smouldering in his eyes.

"Was anyone ever more cross-grained or more foolish?" he asked.

She did not answer and he walked restlessly over the bare floor-boards as he said:

"Have you thought what your life will be like in the future, living in Cornwall with your father going off his head in frustration at not being able to play cards?"

He saw by the expression on Lorinda's face that what he had said struck home.

"No parties, no admirers," he persisted, "unless you count a few clod-hoppers."

He paused, then added almost spitefully:

"In such circumstances, Lorinda, beauty does not last long."

He felt, although he was not sure, that there was almost a stricken look in her eyes, and he went to her and put his arm round her shoulders.

"Come away with me," he said in a low voice. "We

will amuse ourselves one way or another. We might even go to the East, which I have always wished to visit."

She did not move away from him, but he had felt her stiffen at the touch of his arm.

"And when we have exhausted the East?" she asked quietly. "What then?"

"My wife might die. She is not in good health."

Lorinda gave a little laugh and moved away from him.

"Oh, Ulric, that is as much a platitude as saying she does not understand you. People never die when you want them to."

Lord Wroxford looked at her uncertainly. The sunshine coming through the windows glittered on her hair and made it seem as if she was encircled with light.

"God, you are beautiful!" he exclaimed. "I want you, Lorinda! I want you more than I ever believed it possible to want any woman, and I intend to have you!"

Lorinda gave him a glance of sheer mischief.

"My old Nanny used to say, 'Want must be your master,' and that is my answer."

"You cannot mean that!" he said. "You cannot be such a damned fool as to turn down the only sensible offer you will receive in your present circumstances."

His eyes narrowed as he went on:

"I have heard about Edward being taken to the country, while the other gallants who flung themselves at your feet are looking for someone else to idolise."

He saw the smile on Lorinda's lips and it infuriated him.

"I am a very rich man, Lorinda, and I am prepared to spend every penny of my wealth on you. Can you really be so incredibly stupid as to refuse me?"

"I thought we should get down to your money sooner or later," Lorinda said scornfully. "If I were up for sale tomorrow, I am quite certain you would bid for me. Perhaps you would get me cheap! But, as the decision lies with me, I am not interested."

"If I were in my right mind," Lord Wroxford said bitterly, "I would leave you without another word. As it is, I will give you one more chance. Will you come away with me?"

Lorinda put out her hands.

"Dear Ulric, I shall always remember that you made me an offer of some sort, which is more than anyone else has done."

"You really persist in saying no?"

"When I am sitting in the wilds of Cornwall, staring at the sea and wondering where our next crust of bread is coming from, I shall doubtless think of your wealth and be so glad that you still have not enough money to buy me."

"What do you mean by that?" Lord Wroxford enquired.

"I mean that in plain fact you have nothing to offer which I want, nothing for which I would sell myself."

"I do not understand you."

"Which is perhaps a good thing. Good-bye Ulric."

"Do you really mean that?"

"I mean it. Thank you for coming to see me."

As if he could no longer control himself Lord Wroxford stepped forward and reached out his arms, but somehow she managed to elude him.

"Now you are being tiresome," Lorinda said sharply. "Go away, Ulric, I have a lot to do and I cannot waste any more time."

"Damn you!" he swore. "I am serious. You cannot turn me off like this!"

"You can let yourself out."

As she spoke, Lorinda opened the Library door and passed through it. Lord Wroxford heard her running up the uncarpeted stairs.

He stood for a moment, wearing an expression not only of frustration but also of genuine surprise.

He had been confident that Lorinda would accept his proposition rather than bury herself in the wilds of Cornwall.

He waited for a few moments as if he half-expected her to come back. But there was only silence, and walking heavily across the Hall he let himself out the front door.

* * *

The Sale was better attended than even the Auctioneer had hoped. Although it was not to begin until eleven o'clock in the morning, people were already streaming into the house an hour earlier.

The Auction was to be held in the large Salon and the chairs that had been arranged were all occupied long before the Sale began.

Lorinda was well aware that half the people present had come out of curiosity.

She recognised a number of her enemies and knew that they were gloating over the position in which she found herself.

There were those whom she had snubbed and ignored, those who had deprecated the manner in which she behaved, and a number who had secretly admired her for doing what they themselves would never have had the courage to do.

And there were also, she thought with satisfaction, a number of genuine Dealers and Buyers who in competition with one another would keep the prices high.

"Do you really intend to be present, M'Lady?" the Auctioneer had asked.

"I will be there!" Lorinda replied.

"I thought perhaps you'd feel uncomfortable," he said. "On most occasions like this, everything is left entirely to us."

"I am anxious to see how the bidding goes."

She knew that most people would think it extraordinary of her to attend the Sale, but her pride would not let her run away as her father had done.

"They can think what they like," she told herself, "but I will not allow them to believe I am downtrodden or sobbing helplessly on my bed."

She looked defiant and very beautiful as, wearing a becoming gown and a wide-brimmed hat trimmed with feathers, she sat near the Auctioneer and noted the purchaser of every lot.

She actually felt indifferent and impersonal about

the various items, until her mother's jewellery was
brought into the room.

Then for the first time she felt a twinge of regret
and what she impatiently told herself was sheer senti-
ment.

"You glitter like a fairy, Mama," she had said to her
mother as a child when she came to her room to say
good-night before going down to dinner.

"This necklace belonged to my great-great-grand-
mother," her mother had said, touching the emeralds
which encircled her neck. "One day, darling, they will
be yours, and they will match your eyes."

Lorinda looked at the emeralds now and was sorry
she had never worn them.

She had felt they were too ostentatious to be worn
by a young girl, and she prided herself on her good
taste in dress.

She had, however, often thought of the emeralds,
and when she had fetched smaller pieces of jewellery
from the safe she had told herself that the moment she
was married she would wear the emerald necklace.

It would look spectacular against her white skin and
the big stones would glitter beneath her ears.

Now they were to go "under the hammer" and she
looked round the Salon wondering which of the wom-
en present would do them justice.

She was well aware that she need not have put
them in the Sale. They belonged to her and ever since
her mother's death she had refused to allow her father
to sell them or pawn them as he had often wished to
do.

"They are mine, Papa," she said whenever he suggested it. "They belonged to Mama's family and are
therefore nothing to do with the Cambornes."

"Let me raise some money on them, Lorinda," her
father would plead at times. "I will soon win them
back."

But Lorinda had always refused, and although now
she had put them in the Sale she had done so simply
because she was ashamed that he should try to evade
a debt of honour.

When finally the emeralds were knocked down, she felt as if a part of her youth, like her ideals, had gone forever.

They had meant something very special to her, even though she could not exactly put into words what that was, and she felt relieved that they had not been bought by one of her social acquaintances.

An elderly man at the back of the room who looked like a superior clerk had purchased them and she imagined he was a jeweller who would sell them again.

'At least I shall not have to watch anyone gloating over them,' Lorinda thought, and longed for the Sale to come to an end.

When finally it did so, she knew that she was unspeakably relieved.

"A very satisfactory result, if I might say so, M'Lady," the Auctioneer remarked when they were alone in the empty Salon.

"How much does it come to altogether?" Lorinda enquired.

"About forty-five thousand pounds, M'Lady, and if you accept twenty thousand that's been offered for the house this morning, that'll give you a total sum of sixty-five thousand pounds, before our commission's been deducted."

"I have already instructed you to pay the cheque to The Right Honourable Charles Fox."

"It shall be done, M'Lady."

Lorinda picked up her travelling-cape and put it over her shoulders.

"Your Ladyship is leaving?" the Auctioneer enquired.

"Yes, I am leaving," Lorinda repeated.

She walked away without a backward glance.

The travelling-chariot was waiting outside the door, and in charge of it was a very young groom whom she had chosen to accompany her because his wages were lower than those of any of the others.

The chariot was filled with trunks, boxes, valises, and a miscellaneous collection of brass sauce-pans and kitchen utensils, which were not worth putting in the Sale.

Lorinda looked at it, then with a smile she climbed up onto the box and picked up the reins.

There were not many people still outside the house, but nevertheless as she drove away from Hanover Square she was quite certain that before dinner-time the *Beau Monde* would be titillated by the final audacious escapade of Lady Lorinda Camborne.

There was quite a crowd of passers-by to stare in astonishment as they saw her drive down Piccadilly.

They were used to the flamboyant livery of the servants of the aristocracy, but who had ever seen a Lady of Quality with feathers in her hat driving a travelling-chariot and managing it with an unmistakable expertise?

The two horses being fresh, they travelled at a good speed through the traffic and increased their pace even more once they were on the open road.

When there was no longer anyone to see her, Lorinda handed the groom the reins.

"Hold these for a moment, Ben," she said. "We have a long way to go and I might as well be comfortable."

He took the reins as she commanded and Lorinda took off her feather-trimmed hat. She stuffed it under the box-seat, then put a scarf over her red hair and tied it under her chin.

She put out her hands for the reins and as he relinquished them the young groom smiled at her.

"'Tis a bit of an adventure, isn't it, M'Lady?" he asked with a grin.

"It is an adventure into the unknown, Ben," Lorinda agreed. "And as there will be no going back, we might as well enjoy it."

As she spoke she looked at the blue horizon which lay to the south-west.

She knew that she had spoken the truth in what she had said to Ben: "There will be no going back."

This was the end of a chapter in her life.

* * *

It was a long journey and Lorinda was aware of feeling tired of it long before they reached Cornwall.

Because she did not wish to exchange her horses at the Posting-Inns, it meant they could not travel as far as she would have liked every day.

They had to arrive early and give the horses a long rest before they could start off the following morning.

Because she had to economise, Lorinda did not patronise the large and expensive Inns, but the smaller and less-comfortable ones, where her arrival caused a commotion simply because clients of the Quality were rare.

She found however that most Landlords were anxious to please, and in fact, however uncomfortable the bed or coarse the sheets, she managed to sleep deeply and wake refreshed and full of energy in the morning.

She changed from the best gown she had worn at the Sale into something plainer and more serviceable. She had indeed considered making herself really comfortable by wearing male attire.

Then she remembered that for her to appear dressed as a boy would scandalise the majority of the country-folk whom she encountered.

She therefore remained looking feminine, even if the manner in which she disdained a hat seemed surprising to many of the Inn-Keepers and their wives.

Some of the roads were bad but the weather was dry and at least the wheels of the somewhat cumbersome chariot did not get stuck in the thick mud which was one of the worst hazards of travelling in the winter.

There were showers of rain, but Lorinda refused Ben's suggestion that she should sit inside while he drove; for she considered her cape, which had a hood, was sufficient protection against the elements.

Some days it was very hot and the flies bothered the horses, so Lorinda would stop and rest for an hour after their midday meal.

She did not talk much to Ben, but would sit thinking

of what lay ahead and finding it difficult not to worry over how they would ever find the forty thousand pounds that was still owed to Charles Fox.

She was certain that he would not press them for a little while, since he was known as a good-natured man, and having himself been faced with gambling debts, he knew how difficult it was to find quickly large amounts of ready money.

But eventually, Lorinda told herself, her father must get clear of his obligation—the difficulty was how it could be done.

When they had driven over bleak, arid, rocky Bodmin Moor she felt as if she had stepped into a new world.

She had not been in the sheltered estuary of the Fal for many years and she had forgotten how beautiful it was and how breath-taking the flowers were compared with those anywhere else in the country.

The warm climate which at times could be semi-tropical made it possible, as Lorinda remembered now, to grow flowers and plants that could not be grown elsewhere in England.

At this time of the year they were more profuse and more colourful than at any other time.

With a feeling of delight Lorinda recognised orange and lemon trees and even in one place a banana tree.

Beneath them the grass was brilliant with every flower she was able to name, and the wild orchids in their pinks and purples brought back memories of her childhood.

They had lived in Cornwall a great deal when her mother was alive, and it was only after she was dead that her father had refused to leave London.

The Priory had been shut up ever since, except, Lorinda knew, for a couple who acted as caretakers and were content with a pittance because they were grateful for having a roof over their heads.

Feeling quite certain that they would not be able to look after her father to his satisfaction, she had given the groom who had gone with him many instructions as to what should be done.

She thought he would welcome her arrival if for no other reason than because she would be able to make things so much more comfortable for him.

The horses rounded the top of the hill, and as she looked down in the valley below she pointed with her whip and said to Ben:

"There is the Priory!"

There was a touch of pride in Lorinda's voice because it was so beautiful.

The old house had been an ancient Priory attached to a Castle which had decayed into ruins over the centuries.

Gleaming white against the green trees which surrounded it, it looked very majestic as if it defied times and change, beyond vividly blue was the sea.

"Cor, M'Lady, is that yer 'ome?" Ben asked in awe-struck tones.

"It is!" Lorinda replied, and knew as she spoke that it would not be so impressive close to.

That was very evident, she found, as they drove down the long drive which was full of pot-holes and lined with trees long past their prime and sadly in need of attention.

As they reached the end there was a quick impression of the Priory looking very grand and impressive until as they drew nearer still they could see how much of it was in ruins.

The court-yard in front of the door was green with weeds and part of the railings which had once been gilt-tipped had fallen down. The wrought-iron gate which had stood for centuries hung askew from its hinges.

Lorinda drew up the coach outside the front door, conscious that her arms were aching from the long distance they had travelled. Although she was not prepared to admit it, she was thankful they did not have to go any farther.

She stepped down as the groom who had accompanied her father appeared, followed by the elderly couple who she guessed were the caretakers.

She greeted them and walked into the house.

The dilapidation and deterioration was even worse than she had feared. The walls were stained with damp and the ceilings did not bear looking at.

The furniture had obviously not been polished for years, and when she looked into the first room she came to it was evident that it had never been dusted.

She walked on, guessing that her father would be occupying the room which her mother had always liked best and which had large windows opening into the garden, and a beautiful marble fireplace.

As she expected, her father was there, sitting in an armchair, a card-table in front of him.

He was playing Patience.

"I am here, Papa."

Her father did not get up but merely looked at her and she realised he had been drinking.

"And as you see I have arrived safely," Lorinda said, "and since you are so interested, the journey was comparatively comfortable and uneventful!"

"Have you brought me any money?" the Earl enquired.

"Every penny realised by the Sale was sent, as you should have known, to Mr. Charles Fox."

"All of it?"

"Of course!"

"That was a damned silly thing to do," the Earl remarked. "What do you think we are going to live on?"

"I have not really thought about it," Lorinda replied coldly. "I have a few pounds for our immediate needs and I hope there will be something to eat in the garden."

"There are plenty of weeds, if you relish those."

Lorinda walked to the window and looked at the jungle that had once been a beautiful garden.

The green lawns, which had had a surface like velvet, were now overgrown, the flowers and shrubs were a tropical wilderness—a profusion of colour and growth without any semblance of shape or order.

And yet the sun was shining and she could not help feeling that she had come home.

She walked out into the sunshine and almost expected to hear her mother's voice calling to her.

Then, as if she did not wish to remember the past, she walked back into the room where her father was sitting.

"I will go and explore the house," she said, "and I would like to dine early. I am hungry. I have had nothing to eat since breakfast."

"The food is disgusting!" the Earl said. "There is no-one in the house who can cook, and I—"

Lorinda did not wait for the end of his sentence. She started to explore the house and found it even more horrifying than she had anticipated.

"I hope this is edible," the Earl said at dinner as he helped himself from a dish offered to him by the old caretaker.

"I cooked most of it myself," Lorinda said. "Tomorrow I will give Mrs. Dogman some lessons so that at least we will not be hungry."

"It certainly tastes better than what I have had to endure these last few days," her father remarked grudgingly.

"Have you tried shooting a rabbit or two?" Lorinda enquired. "I saw quite a number of them as I came through the Park."

"I have not found a gun yet," her father replied.

"What have you been doing, Papa?"

"I have been down to the village."

"Doubtless to visit the Penryn Arms," Lorinda remarked.

"Where else is there to go?" he enquired. "I could not even find a drink in the house."

He paused before he added:

"At least they have excellent brandy!"

Lorinda looked surprised and he explained:

"From France—where else?"

"You mean it is smuggled?"

"As it always has been—the Cornish do not alter their ways."

Lorinda was silent and after a moment he said reflectively:

"We might try a little smuggling ourselves! They tell me that those engaged in it are making a fortune, sometimes multiplying their original investment five times over!"

"Can that be true?" Lorinda asked.

She remembered now that the villagers had always been engaged in or concerned with smuggling. She had understood that the rewards were well worth the risk, but this profit seemed fantastic.

"Smuggling would at least relieve the monotony of this dead-alive hole," the Earl remarked.

He spoke aggressively and because Lorinda had no wish to antagonise him she asked:

"They must have been surprised to see you in the village. Are there many changes since we were last here?"

"None that I can see," her father answered, "except that a great number of people are dead and the rest look as if they ought to be."

Lorinda laughed.

"Cheer up, Papa. It may not be Carlton House or White's, but it is home and as we have to live here we might as well make the best of it."

"There is no 'best' as far as I can see," the Earl grumbled.

"I cannot remember them clearly," Lorinda said, "but we must have had some neighbours in the past."

"If there are I have not met them as yet."

"I do not suppose they know you are here. Try to remember their names."

Her father shrugged his shoulders as if he was not interested. Then he said, as if reluctant to impart the information:

"There is one thing that is new."

"What is that?" Lorinda enquired.

"Some fool, and he must be one, is renovating Penryn Castle!"

"I do not believe it!" Lorinda exclaimed. "Is it one of the Penryns?"

"No—I understand his name is Hayle—Durstan Hayle, and he comes from India."

"He must be very rich if he can afford to restore the Castle," Lorinda said. "I remember it as being even more dilapidated than this house."

"They say in the village that he is rolling in money. I wonder if he plays cards. . . ."

"Now . . . Papa!" Lorinda admonished. "You know you cannot play until your debt is cleared."

"And how are we likely to clear it?" the Earl enquired. "The only way I know of making money is to gamble."

"You cannot gamble if you have nothing to gamble with," Lorinda said as if she were speaking to a child.

"If this Indian chap wants to play, I shall damned well play with him," the Earl replied. "I might be able to take a bit of money off him."

Lorinda drew in her breath.

'It is no use arguing,' she thought.

She would never make her father see how wrong and indeed dishonourable it was of him to wish to gamble when he had not yet paid back the money he owed.

"I shall certainly want to look at Penryn Castle," she said aloud. "What have you found out about Mr. Hayle?"

"Just that he is warm in the pocket," the Earl replied.

"I wonder why he is interested in the Castle. Most men who have made their money in the East want to be in London or near it."

"I expect he will make a mess of whatever he is doing," the Earl said gloomily. "I remember when I was a boy the Castle was one of the finest show-places in the whole country!"

The Earl paused.

"There used to be Balls in the winter, garden-parties in the summer, and old Lord Penryn entertained with a lavishness one never sees today."

He sound quite animated and to encourage him Lorinda said:

"You must have had a lot of fun in those days, Papa."

"I will tell you one thing—we had damned good horses!" the Earl remarked. "And when Penryn came into the title, he and I used to organise steeple-chases. Great fun they were! Although several of the riders broke their necks!"

He gave an exasperated sigh.

"I do not suppose this damned fellow knows one end of a horse from the other. More used to riding elephants!"

He spoke disparagingly and Lorinda knew it was because he resented Mr. Hayle having money while they were impoverished.

Her father could be very petty-minded at times, and she hoped for his sake that he was not going to start a feud with his new neighbour even before they knew him.

Unless the county had changed a great deal since she was a child, she was quite certain that their neighbours were few and far between, and whatever the newcomer was like, they would be wise to make the best of him.

'Perhaps he is Papa's age,' she thought to herself, 'but I hope he is not a hard drinker. We cannot afford large wine bills!'

When dinner was finished she walked with her father back into the Sitting-Room and as she did so she started to plan how she would make at least that room if none other in the house comfortable.

There would be no sense in opening up many rooms with only the old couple to keep them clean. So the best thing to do would be to amalgamate the best pieces of furniture and the most comfortable sofas and chairs and shut up the rest of the house.

As if he knew what she was thinking, her father suddenly said almost violently:

"I cannot stand this, Lorinda! I cannot stand being incarcerated here, miles from anywhere, with no-one to talk to and only a few yokels with whom to have a drink."

There was so much pain in his voice that for the first time Lorinda felt sorry for him.

"There is nothing we can do about it, Papa," she answered. "Here we have to stay, unless we can sell the house and grounds. I put it in the hands of the Agents before I left London, but needless to say they were not very hopeful."

Her father did not speak and after a moment she went on:

"As soon as I have time I will go to Falmouth and see if there is an Estate Agent there and perhaps we can put an advertisement in the local newspaper."

She expected an outburst from her father and for him to rage against the idea as he had done when they were in London.

Instead he said apathetically:

"Do what you like! I only know that if I have to stick with this for long I really shall put a bullet through my head!"

He flung himself down in the armchair and as he did so knocked over the table, and the cards with which he had been playing Patience went flying all over the room.

As if they broke the last strands of his self-control, the Earl started to swear.

His oaths were violent and many of them were coarse.

Lorinda did not wait to listen. She walked out through the open window and into the garden.

The sun was sinking in a blaze of glory and the sky was crimson and gold.

She heard the high squeak of a bat and looked up to see its sharp pointed wings silhouetted against the sky.

She walked farther away from the house until she could no longer hear her father's voice and then drew a deep breath.

"I will not let this defeat me," she said aloud defiantly, but her voice was lost in the thick branches of the trees.

CHAPTER THREE

It was dark in the wood and only a very faint gleam from the starlit sky came through the branches of the trees.

Lorinda thought, however, that she would have known her way blindfolded along the twisting little path which led from the Priory grounds through the thick woods towards the sea.

She stumbled once and heard the clink of coins in the pocket of her coat, and thought with satisfaction that if her father was right they would be increased one-hundred-fold before she handled them again.

It was a desperate venture that she had decided upon, but she felt it was forced upon her because there was in fact no other way they could live.

The money she had brought from London was not going to last long and she saw that in a very short time they would be completely dependent on what they could grow in the garden or shoot in the grounds.

There would certainly not be enough money for the drink her father could not do without, and she was quite certain that he had already run up a large bill at the Penryn Arms.

She had thought while driving down from London

that there would be rents coming in from the tenants
who lived on the Estate.

She had envisaged, although she knew it was a for-
lorn hope, that there might be some outstanding
debts which could be collected so that they could
start off on a firm financial foundation.

The rents were certainly in arrears, but when
Lorinda visited the tenants she had not the courage
to ask them for what they owed.

They in fact presented her with a long list of re-
pairs which should have been the Landlord's re-
sponsibility, and she could see without being told
that the roofs of the houses and barns were in a
disgraceful state of disrepair.

There would therefore be no income from the
tenants. How then could they live?

Lorinda had always been prepared to take the
courageous, if not the outrageous, action, and the
smugglers seemed to supply both.

She had kept her money carefully hidden from her
father, but now from the diminishing hoard she took
twenty golden guineas and by making discreet en-
quiries found out where the smugglers landed when
they returned from the long trip to the French coast.

As soon as she was told that it was Keverne Cove
she remembered it well from the old days—a small,
discreet inlet amongst the high cliffs which surrounded it, where she had often picnicked with her
mother or her Nurse.

As Lorinda proceeded the sky began to lighten and
the stars to fade.

She knew that the dawn was not far away, and
she guessed that the smugglers would approach under cover of darkness to avoid the coast-guards and
land in the cove as soon as the first light of dawn
made it possible for them.

She walked on, wondering whether any of the
men would remember her.

But was sure that when she told them who she
was, they would be only too willing to oblige her by
taking her money and buying with it the brandy,

tobacco, laces, and silks which fetched such large prices in the English markets.

Smuggling was part of a Cornishman's blood, and he did not only do it for gain but for the excitement it brought him and to gratify his inherent inclination to take risks.

Now there was the scuttle of small animals amongst the undergrowth, the flutter of birds moving off the roost.

As Lorinda progressed a little farther she could hear the sound of the waves breaking against the cliffs, mingling with the song of the waking birds.

Sure-footed, she walked on, finding it easy to move as she was unhampered by a skirt.

She had always preferred men's attire, and she found in the trunks stored away in the attics of the Priory a lot of her father's clothes which he had worn as a boy.

The full-skirted coats were quite impractical, but the breeches, which fitted Lorinda to perfection, were just what was needed on such an adventure as this.

She found a coat to cover her thin lawn shirt, and although old and dilapidated it fitted well over her shoulders.

Because she thought it would be wise to appear dressed like a boy until the smugglers learnt otherwise, she piled her red-gold hair into a black velvet peaked cap which might have been worn by one of her grandfather's out-riders.

She had a glance at herself in the mirror before she left her room and thought that in fact she looked quite masculine and only on closer inspection would the beauty of her face betray her.

Now the sound of the waves grew louder, the trees became sparser, and to her left she could see the jagged outline of the cliffs.

The ground began to slope down towards the cove but she kept in the shelter of the trees, thinking that when the smugglers arrived they might be frightened off if they saw someone waiting for them.

There was also the possibility that, suspected of

being a spy or a coast-guard, she would receive a
bullet in her body before she could explain her mis-
sion.

The undergrowth grew thicker down the slope, but
now at last Lorinda could see the cove quite clearly.

The inlet between the cliffs which stretched in-
land for quite a considerable way was a perfect hid-
ing-place for smugglers' boats, and was quite indis-
cernible from the sea.

But from where she came to a standstill it was easy
to be aware that the cove was empty and the smugglers had not yet arrived.

She put her hand into her pocket to make sure
that the bag of gold was still there, and leaning
against the trunk of a tree she waited.

Now the stars had almost faded and the first translucent light of dawn gave everything an ethereal
beauty that was almost indescribable.

Suddenly with a leap of her heart Lorinda saw a
black spot on the sea coming nearer and still nearer
until it slid into the mouth of the cove and moved
to the further end of it, close to where she stood
watching.

The boat was long and narrow and had twenty
oarsmen.

She could see their heads quite clearly against the
grey sky, but their faces were still in darkness and
as she watched she realised how quiet they were.

The men did not speak, and although she saw
them ship their oars they did it silently.

Two men in the bow jumped out into the water to
drag the boat onto the stony beach.

Lorinda could see that the stern was piled high
with merchandise. Then a movement on the land attracted her attention.

Looking higher up in the wood, she saw a number of small ponies led by boys proceeding towards
the cove.

All the men had now disembarked from the boat
and she thought that this was her moment to speak
to them.

She stepped forward, then opened her lips to give a cry of sheer terror, which was muffled before she could make it.

A hand covered her mouth and an arm as hard as steel encircled her body.

She had heard no-one approach, and the shock of being held made her for a moment rigid with astonishment.

Then she began to fight.

She struggled and kicked and twisted and turned her body, without avail.

The arm which encircled her was so tight that it made it difficult for her to breathe and the hand which covered her mouth was almost brutal in its strength.

She fought silently and desperately and it was even more frightening that it might have been because she could not see her captor. She knew only that he was there and that she was helpless in his grasp.

Her struggles dislodged the cap she wore and her hair cascaded over her shoulders in a red wave.

It was then for the first time that her captor made a sound.

He gave a low laugh and to Lorinda it was even more frightening than if he had sworn at her.

She suddenly felt exhausted with the effort she had made to free herself. She had fought desperately but her struggles had made not the slightest impression.

Now because she was breathless her body sagged against him and the man said in a low voice:

"This sort of work is not for you. Go home!"

She was infuriated by the note of authority in his voice.

She began to struggle again, knowing even as she did so that it would be quite ineffectual.

He picked her up in his arms, and although when her feet were off the ground she tried to kick back at him, it made no difference.

He carried her back the way she had come, and when they reached the thickest part of the trees where the daylight had not yet percolated he set her down on her feet.

"Go home!" he said. "And keep your money for some better purpose."

He took his hand from her mouth as he spoke and as he did so she realised how much it had hurt her.

Dark though it was, she wanted to turn round and confront him.

But his hands on her shoulders were pushing her forward, and because for the moment she seemed to have no alternative she went the way he wished her to go.

She walked for a few yards. Then, rebellious at the thought that she was obeying a stranger's instructions, furiously resentful at the manner in which she had been treated, she turned round.

It was very dark in the wood and it was almost impossible to see even the outline of the tree-trunks.

She stared back, thinking that if he had stood still after dismissing her she must be able to see him, but she could see nothing.

There was no sign of a man nor had she heard any movement.

She stood there, indecisive, wondering whether she should defy him and go back to the smugglers.

Then she wondered if perhaps he was one of their band.

How else could he have guessed that it was money she had brought with her—money which she wished them to invest for her on their next journey to France?

She stood for some minutes, uncertain what it would be best for her to do.

Then she was aware of how much he had hurt her mouth and chin how the constriction of his arm round her body made her feel as if he had bruised, if not broken, her ribs.

In a battle of strength she would have no chance and therefore must accept the inevitable.

She was seething with an anger that she could not suppress. For the first time in her life she had been defeated and prevented from doing what she intended to do.

It was even more galling to realise that not only was her opponent and enemy a stranger, but she had not the slightest idea what he looked like.

* * *

Lorinda came from the stables with her cheeks glowing and a smile on her lips.

She had just ridden back to the Priory after spending the morning breaking in a wild colt for a farmer who was one of their tenants.

He told her that he had bought it at the Horse Fair which had taken place in Falmouth the previous week, and only when he got it home did he find that it was completely unmanageable.

" 'Twere cheap enough, M'Lady," he said in his broad accent, "but now Oi reckons Oi've wasted me money."

"I will break it in for you," Lorinda said, a sudden light in her eyes.

"Oi'd be roight grateful, M'Lady, but Oi'd not wish ye to break yer neck."

"I will not do that," Lorinda assured him confidently.

It had been a tussle which had lasted for over two hours, at the end of which there was no doubt that Lorinda was the victor.

There was still a great deal to do, but the colt was already beginning to acknowledge her mastery and she knew that it would not take long before he responded to her commands.

As she reached the front of the house she saw that outside stood an extremely smart Phaeton drawn by a pair of chestnut horses which made her draw in her breath in admiration.

There was a groom at their heads and Lorinda realised that their owner must be in the house with her father.

She quickened her step as she moved across the Hall, wondering who could be calling.

It never struck her that it might be a good idea to

change from the riding-breeches she was wearing,
which had belonged to her father, and the black riding-boots with their silver spurs.

It was a hot day and she wore only a boy's shirt
with a silk handkerchief tied round her neck.

It was a sensible costume in which to school a wild
horse, but she knew that the farmer had looked at
her in surprise and she thought that the sooner they
got used to her appearance the better.

It would have been impossible for her to do what
she had done this morning hampered by a lady's
riding-habit and sitting side-saddle.

Her hair was drawn back in a chignon which had
been tight when she had started on her struggle with
the colt, but now strands of hair had come loose and
were curling round her oval forehead.

Without a thought, however, for her appearance,
Lorinda opened the door of the Sitting-Room.

As she had expected, her father was not alone, and
the two men were standing at the window talking
together.

They turned at her entrance and Lorinda saw that
the visitor was a tall man with broad shoulders, and
somehow, although she could not understand it, she
thought he was different from any man she had ever
seen before.

He was not exactly handsome, but he had an ar-
resting face and she saw that below the strongly
marked eye-brows his dark eyes were keen and ob-
servant.

He certainly stared at her in a manner which she
vaguely thought was more impertinent than admiring, and as she advanced there was something
cynical in the faint smile on his firm lips, which she
resented.

"Oh, there you are, Lorinda!" her father said. "You
were asking about Mr. Durstan Hayle, and here he is
in person!"

Lorinda held out her hand.

"How do you do?"

His clasp was hard and as he looked at her she

thought for the first time that she should have changed into a gown.

For one thing, he would expect her to curtsey, and she could hardly do that in riding-breeches.

"I have been breaking in a colt for Farmer Trevin," she said, then was annoyed with herself for feeling that an explanation was necessary.

Instinctively her chin went up and there was a look of defiance in her eyes as she met those of Mr. Hayle.

Something obviously amused him before he looked away from her to her father.

"I will leave you now, My Lord, to think over the proposition I have made to you. Let me know your decision this evening, or at the latest tomorrow morning."

"What proposition?" Lorinda asked.

"Your father will tell you what I have proposed when I have left," Durstan Hayle answered.

His reply made Lorinda furious.

Yet after all he was not to know that it would be impossible for her father to decide anything without consulting her.

"I would like to hear what this is all about," she insisted.

Mr. Hayle's eyes flickered over her and once again she sensed that there was something impertinent in the manner in which he obviously criticised her.

He held out his hand to the Earl.

"I shall be interested to hear what you decide, My Lord," he said, and walked from the room without another glance at Lorinda.

She stared after him in astonishment.

This was certainly not the way men usually behaved when they met her, and she found it even more infuriating when she realised that there was a distinction about him which she had not expected to find in the country.

His clothes were fashionable and well cut but he wore them with a carelessness that made them a part of him and which told her that he was supremely sure of himself and not concerned with the opinions of other people.

She did not question how she knew so much about him. She just felt it instinctively, and as the door closed and she and her father were alone she said with an unexpected sharpness:

"What has he been proposing to you, Papa?"

To her surprise, the Earl walked across the room to seat himself in an armchair before he replied.

He seemed unable to find the right words and Lorinda looked at him apprehensively.

"Well?" she asked. "It is obviously something unusual or your visitor would not have been so secretive about it."

She spoke scornfully and her father seemed to have difficulty in looking at her. After a moment she moved close to him to say firmly:

"Tell me, Papa. I have to know sooner or later."

"Hayle has offered to buy the Priory and the Estate!"

Lorinda's eyes lit up.

"That will be the answer to all our problems! What has he offered?"

"Eighty thousand pounds!"

"Did you say eighty thousand?" She gasped. "He must be mad! It is not worth half that!"

"He pointed out to me that forty thousand would pay the debt I owe to Charles Fox and give me the other forty thousand for myself. It is a generous offer, you must agree, Lorinda."

"Of course it is generous! The man must be a lunatic or for some reason determined to splash his money round. You accepted, of course?"

"I thought I should first talk it over with you."

"Knowing I would agree," Lorinda said. "It is everything we have hoped for and a great deal more. You will be out of debt, Papa, and if we manage carefully we can live extremely well on a capital of forty thousand pounds."

"Hayle suggested that I should go to Ireland," the Earl said. "I did not say anything, of course, but he seemed to know that I would not wish to return to London for the moment."

"How could he know that?" Lorinda asked.

Her father shrugged his shoulders.

"I have no idea, although I did not argue with him. It is true enough."

"No, you cannot go back, even when the debt is paid," Lorinda agreed, "and Ireland is certainly a possibility. The hunting there is fantastic. I shall enjoy that."

There was silence for a moment, then the Earl said:

"You will not be with me."

"I will . . . not be with you? What do you mean?" Lorinda enquired.

"There is a—condition to the sale."

It was obvious that something was very wrong and Lorinda looked at her father in perplexity before she asked:

"What condition?"

"That you should—marry him!"

Lorinda's eyes widened.

For a moment she was completely speechless, then she managed to ejaculate:

"Is this . . . some sort of . . . joke, Papa?"

"No. That was Hayle's offer: that he would buy the Priory and the Estate, and as there is no Camborne to carry on the ancient tradition, he would marry you so that it would thereby remain partly yours."

"He must be mad!" Lorinda cried. "I have never heard of anything so nonsensical in all my life!"

She put out her hand to hold on to the mantelpiece as if she was in need of support before she said:

"I presume you argued with him, Papa? Did you say we would be prepared to sell the house and land for less if I was not included in the deal?"

"He made it quite clear that he would buy only if you became his wife," the Earl said.

"He cannot mean it! He has never met me until this moment, and if he has seen me without my knowing it, he certainly did not look as if he was in any way enamoured of me."

She thought as she spoke that it was hardly surprising, considering the way she was dressed. Then she told herself that if he was shocked it would be all the better.

He must be persuaded to drop this ridiculous idea.

He could have the Priory and the land, if he wanted it, for as little as thirty thousand pounds. Lorinda in fact had not expected as much.

But for her to marry this stranger, this man of whom they knew nothing, was too preposterous a proposal even to be considered.

"I will have to talk to him," she said aloud.

Her father stirred restlessly.

"Hayle made it very clear when he spoke that he wished to deal with me alone. I think he has not much opinion of women having any business acumen."

"Then he will learn that he is mistaken."

"He insists on an answer to his offer either this evening or tomorrow morning. I think he intends to leave the Castle tomorrow afternoon."

"So he is dictating his terms," Lorinda said. "As you well know, Papa, they are absolutely unthinkable!"

Her father rose from his chair.

"Damn it all, Lorinda, you cannot say that. We are not likely to get a better offer, as you well know. Who else is going to give up eighty thousand pounds for this ramshackle ruin and an Estate that needs thousands of pounds spent on it?"

Lorinda knew this was true.

"What is more, it means I can get away," the Earl said. "I cannot stand much more of this! In fact, Lorinda, I swear that if you do not accept this offer I will kill myself as I meant to do if you had not interfered."

He walked to the window.

"I loathe the country without money, without horses, without a house to which I can invite people to stay, and without sporting facilities! I could have all those things in Ireland and play cards with congenial companions."

"And to enable you to do this you would expect me to sacrifice myself?" Lorinda asked sharply.

"You have to marry someone," the Earl answered. "You have refused enough suitors in all conscience. Why the hell did you not get yourself a rich husband when you had the opportunity?"

Lorinda drew in her breath. She had no answer to this.

"If I had done my duty as a father I would have seen to it that you were married off a long time ago," the Earl went on. "Young ladies do not choose their husbands, they are chosen for them. I should have insisted on your taking Dawlish, who is rich enough—"

"But half-witted," Lorinda interposed.

"Or Edward Hinton. At least he comes from a good family," her father continued. "What are you waiting for? The Angel Gabriel to drop down from the skies? The Shah of Persia to offer you his throne? You are only a woman, and like all the rest you need a home and a husband to keep you in order."

"And you think Mr. Hayle will do all that?" Lorinda asked scornfully.

Even as she spoke she remembered the hardness of his eyes as he looked at her and the cynical twist of his lips.

"I will not marry him!" she said. "I will not be slaughtered so that you can have a Roman Holiday!"

There was silence, then her father's eyes narrowed.

"You will marry him," he said. "For once you are not going to defy me, Lorinda, and I will listen to no more arguments."

She would have spoken, but he went on quickly:

"I shall accept Hayle's offer and the marriage will be arranged when it suits him. You talk a great deal about family honour. Well, when I have his money firmly in my pocket, you can do what you like about fulfilling your part of the contract."

As he finished speaking the Earl turned away.

"Papa . . . you cannot do this!" Lorinda cried.

He did not answer her but merely went out of the

room and slammed the door behind him. She sat staring after him before her hands went up to her cheeks.

"I will not marry him! I will not!" Lorinda said over and over again for the rest of the afternoon.

When she saw one of the grooms waiting outside the front door at about five o'clock she knew why he was there.

She stormed into the Sitting-Room and found her father sealing a note he had just written.

He looked up at her and she saw that he had been drinking heavily.

"I have written my acceptance to Hayle's offer," he said, his voice slurred, "and there is not a damned thing you can do about it!"

Lorinda looked at him and realised that in the state he was in it would be useless for her to argue.

For one thing, even if they had a flaming row, it was doubtful whether he would afterwards remember anything they had said to each other.

She made up her mind.

"Give me the note," she said.

"If you tear it up I shall write another one."

"I have no intention of tearing it up," Lorinda answered. "I will take it to Mr. Hayle myself."

She put out her hand and her father handed her the note somewhat reluctantly.

"If you prevent me from having that money to get to Ireland," he said, "I swear I will strangle you! That is what I wanted to do anyway, when you were born!"

"You wanted a son and I disappointed you," Lorinda replied. "It is too late to go over that now, Papa, but it is not too late for me to tell Mr. Hayle exactly what I think of him."

She did not wait for her father's reply but went from the room.

She had changed before tea from her riding-clothes into a becoming afternoon-gown with a full skirt and a white fichu.

She told herself there was no point in changing

again and she merely sent the groom to the stables to
have a side-saddle put on the horse, and told him
that his services would not be required.

It did not worry Lorinda what she wore when she
was riding, and without a hat or gloves and carrying
only a small thin whip she set off in the direction of
Penryn Castle.

Across the fields it was less than two miles from the
Priory, although a much longer distance by road.

The heat of the day had gone and the shadows
were long and purple over the flower-filled grass.

If Lorinda had not been so worried she would have
appreciated the beauty of it, but she was worried and
apprehensive in a manner that was quite different
from anything she had ever felt before.

She had a frightening feeling that she was being
swept along on a tidal wave and there was nothing
she could do to save herself.

It was, she thought, ironic that she, who for two
years had refused every suitor who had laid his heart
at her feet, should now be caught in a trap. It
threatened to force her to the altar when every instinct in her body revolted against it.

"How can he want anything so utterly and incredibly ridiculous?" she asked herself.

She tried to believe that it was, as she had thought
at first, a joke, but there was something about Durstan Hayle which made her feel that he was not a
practical-joker and that what he said he meant.

"I dislike him," she told herself, "and the idea of
being married to him is insupportable."

Long before she neared the Castle she could see it
from a distance.

It had been built on a hill in the days when it was
always wise to be able to see one's enemies ap-
proaching, and it had been in existence for centuries.

The original Castle had been a comparatively small
fortification, but it had been added to over the centuries.

While the original great stone Keep remained, the

house was a mixture of Elizabethan with Queen Anne and early Georgian additions.

It had not, however, been lived in by a Penryn since Lorinda's birth.

The huge empty rooms with their fallen ceilings and twisting staircases, which seemed to have been built only for the habitation of ghosts, had been a joy and a delight in her childhood.

She could remember chasing her friends from room to room, sliding precariously over the roofs and playing Hide-and-Seek in the empty building, where every voice echoed and re-echoed hauntingly.

Now as she drew nearer she saw that the glass had been put back in the windows and the surrounding gardens restored.

The lawns were cut and although it was late in the evening she saw as she rode nearer that there were quite a number of men still working on the flower-beds.

"Money can buy everything!" she told herself scornfully, and thought with a little pang of the wild and overgrown garden at the Priory which had once been her mother's pride.

As she approached the huge brass-studded front door, a groom came hurrying to hold her horse while she dismounted and walked up the steps.

As the door opened she saw the Butler waiting for her, flanked by a number of footmen in livery.

"I wish to speak to Mr. Durstan Hayle," she said in a clear, imperious voice.

"Certainly, Ma'am," the Butler replied. "May I have your name?"

"Lady Lorinda Camborne," she replied, and seeing by the glint in his eyes that he recognised the name she thought he must be Cornish.

He led her with some pomposity across the Hall, which had been restored in a manner which Lorinda could not help admiring.

Now for the first time she could appreciate the wonderful plaster-work which had always been dirty and broken; the alcoves were filled with statues and the carved, curving staircase was no longer full of holes.

The Butler opened the door of a room which had always seemed particularly empty because it had once been a Library but there had only been broken bookcases to remind anyone of it.

For a moment Lorinda was too astonished at the transformation to do anything but stare.

The ceiling had been repainted by a master hand and there were books on all the walls. A magnificent carved-stone mantelpiece which she remembered as being black and dirty with age now gleamed white and the empty fireplace was stacked with flowers.

"Lady Lorinda Camborne, Sir!" the Butler announced, and she saw Mr. Hayle rise from a chair in which he had been sitting reading a newspaper.

She advanced towards him, and, seeing his eyes look at her with the same penetrating expression, she regretted that she had not put a bonnet on her red hair.

She curtseyed and he bowed.

"This is a surprise," he said, "although I rather anticipated that you might wish to speak to me."

"It was obvious, was it not?" Lorinda enquired.

"Will you sit down?"

He indicated a chair and she sat down with an unmistakable grace, though aware that she was holding herself stiffly.

"What can I do for you?" he enquired as he seated himself. "Or is that an unnecessary question?"

"I came to see if you really meant that quite ridiculous proposition you put to my father."

"I cannot think that eighty thousand pounds is ridiculous," Durstan Hayle replied.

"I am not referring to the money which you have offered to buy the Priory," Lorinda said, "but the condition that goes with it."

"I thought perhaps you might resent it," he said with a smile that irritated her.

"Then why make it, if you know I would refuse?"

"If that is your father's answer, Lady Lorinda," Durstan Hayle said, "there is really nothing more for us to discuss."

His voice was cold and he rose to his feet as he spoke.

Lorinda stared at him with wide eyes.

Never had she met, or expected to meet, a man who would behave in such a manner towards her.

"There is a great deal more I wish to say," she remarked after a moment's pause.

"The offer I made to your father was quite clear," Durstan Hayle replied. "It is all—or nothing!"

"But why should you wish to marry me?" Lorinda asked.

"It seems a pity that there should not be a Camborne in, shall we say, partial possession of lands that have been theirs for over five hundred years."

"Is that your real reason for asking me to marry you?"

"I cannot think of a better one," he answered. "The history of Cornwall means a great deal to me."

For perhaps the first time in her life Lorinda felt at a loss.

No man had ever asked her to be his wife in such an uncompromising and indifferent manner.

"What I was going to suggest," she said after a moment, "was that you could have the house and the grounds for a far smaller sum if I was not to be included in the bargain."

"I am not prepared to discuss it," Durstan Hayle said, "and as I told your father, I prefer to do business with a man."

"When the business closely concerns me, I wish to be included."

"Very well, Lady Lorinda. I presume you can understand plain English. My offer remains open until tomorrow morning—after that it will be withdrawn."

"I am asking you to compromise."

"And I am refusing. If you have nothing further to

say on the matter, please allow me to show you to your carriage."

He obviously expected her to rise, but Lorinda remained where she was.

Her mind was in a turmoil. She felt as if she had come up against a brick wall which was unscalable, and yet she did not wish to acknowledge defeat.

Her mind went quickly over every possible way by which she might persuade him to change his mind and compromise as she had suggested.

She realised he was watching her and once again she saw that cynical twisted smile which made her feel, incredibly, although of course it could not be so, that he despised her.

She had the feeling that perhaps he expected her to plead with him; but that, she told herself proudly, she would never do!

He had driven her into a corner and for the moment she could think of no way of escape. However, she was determined not to humble herself, but to defy him in every possible way she could.

"Have you really thought out the consequences of this extraordinary offer?" she asked.

"I am a businessman," Durstan Hayle replied. "I therefore look at any deal I make from every possible angle."

Lorinda disliked the word "deal" where she was concerned.

Facing him, her eyes meeting his, she said:

"You surely cannot contemplate taking as a wife a woman who already dislikes you. For, let me make it quite clear, I think your offer is an insult, and what I have seen already fills me with great apprehension for the future."

"You are very frank," Durstan Hayle said.

"Is there any point in being anything else?" Lorinda asked. "You do not know me and you therefore cannot be aware that I loathe the thought of marriage to any man. I detest men! Although I have had many proposals of marriage during the past two years

I have not been remotely tempted to accept any of them."

"Surely that makes it easier?" he said. "If you were drooling over some young Gallant whom you are unable to marry, it would make the situation between us unpleasant."

"There could be nothing more unpleasant than having to marry a man of whom I know nothing," Lorinda snapped, "and who is apparently quite insensitive to my feelings."

"As obviously you are to mine," he answered.

She made an exasperated sound and rose to her feet.

"Do you really intend to go through with this farce?" she asked. "To marry me because I am a Camborne . . ."

She stopped, then said:

"Is that the reason? Having made your fortune, you want an aristocratic wife? Then let me suggest, Mr. Hayle, there are many women who would accept you and your wealth with the greatest of pleasure. Why not find one of them?"

"Because they have not so obligingly an Estate which, joined to mine, would give me the exact acreage I require," Durstan Hayle replied.

There was something in the way he spoke which made Lorinda long to scream at him, even to hit him.

How could any man be so insufferably smug and pleased with himself, and be so superior when he had nothing to be superior about?

"You can have the land," she said, "but why not set your sights a little higher? Surely you will not be content with the daughter of an impoverished Earl? I am sure you could find one whose father wears a Ducal coronet. Then all the doors of Society would be open to you."

"It is of course an idea," Durstan Hayle said coolly, "but I have chosen you."

He might be a Sultan conferring his favours upon a Concubine, Lorinda thought furiously.

She stood in front of him, the anger smoldering in her green eyes, and felt as if there was a tumult taking place within her breast beneath the frilled white fichu which encircled her shoulders.

"Is it yes—or no?" Durstan Hayle asked quietly.

Lorinda longed to throw his offer in his face, to tear up the note her father had given her, to tell him to go to hell.

Then she remembered how very little money they had left and that if her father had to face poverty and the loneliness of the Priory, he might really put his threat into action and take his life.

Slowly, hating the man standing in front of her with a violence she did not know she possessed, Lorinda drew her father's note from the pocket in her skirt.

For a moment she thought wildly that she was signing her own death warrant, or committing herself to a prison from which there was no escape and in which she would suffer the tortures of the damned.

Then with an air of pride that she was far from feeling she held the note out in front of her.

"Here is my father's acceptance of your offer," she said scornfully. "But make no mistake, I loathe the thought of it and the idea of marriage makes me feel physically sick!"

Durstan Hayle took the note from her and bowed ironically.

"Your decision is a wise one, but you really had little alternative," he said.

Lorinda did not deign to answer but walked across the floor and waited until he opened the door for her.

She walked ahead in silence. There was the same array of flunkeys in the Hall, and without saying good-bye she passed through the front door and down the steps to where her horse was waiting.

She only hoped that Durstan Hayle was surprised at the manner in which she had come to visit him.

A groom helped her into the saddle, then digging in her spurs she made her horse spring forward in a spirited manner, his hoofs raising a shower of gravel.

She did not look back, but she had the uncomfortable yet unmistakable feeling that Durstan Hayle was watching her with that cynical, mocking twist to his lips.

CHAPTER FOUR

Lorinda stood at her window, looking out at the Park.

It was a day of brilliant sunshine and the riot of flowers in the garden were a flash of colour against the green of the overgrown yew-hedges and the more delicate shrubs.

She had awakened with a feeling that something ominous was about to happen and remembered as if being struck by lightning that it was her wedding-day.

She had not been able to sleep until late last night and even then she had thought that perhaps a miracle would save her and that today would never come.

But now there was less than an hour before her father would take her to the little grey Church, where she had been christened, to marry her to a man she hated.

She had not seen Durstan Hayle since she had gone to the Castle to confront him, only to suffer defeat at his hands.

He had been away, where she did not know, but the arrangements for the marriage had gone ahead and she had been informed by his Agent exactly what was to take place.

After the ceremony in the Church, which was to be performed by the Vicar, they would proceed to the Castle for the wedding-breakfast, at which all the important personages in the county would be present.

Lorinda had no idea who these were and she would not condescend to ask the Agent for information.

She had the idea, however, that there would not be many of them.

After the wedding-breakfast was over they would meet the tenants and the employees, who would have a special feast in the great Tithe barn which Lorinda remembered as being roofless but which had now apparently been repaired.

Afterwards when dusk came there would be fireworks and dancing on the lawn, in which the Morris dancers would be the high spot of the evening.

She would have expressed disapproval of the arrangements and been openly contemptuous had not her father exclaimed delightedly over and over again that they were just what had taken place in the past and he remembered exactly the same sort of celebrations when he was a child.

Lorinda had no personal message from her future husband, but whenever she thought of him she felt her dislike of him grow until she was almost frightened by the intensity of her feelings.

"I hate him! I hate him!" she told herself, and knew that the trap she had feared had closed round her and after today she would have no escape.

She was already dressed in the gown she intended to wear at her wedding.

Early that morning, soon after she had awakened, the elderly Mrs. Dogman had struggled up the stairs with a huge box which she informed Lorinda had been delivered by a carriage from the Castle.

Even before she opened it Lorinda suspected what it was, and when she raised the lid and looked inside she discovered that she was not mistaken.

Durstan Hayle had sent her a wedding-gown!

It was in fact one of the most beautiful gowns she had ever seen and she was well aware how much it would become her.

Of dead white satin covered with fragile white gauze, its purity would enhance the translucence of her skin, and her hair would be vividly red under the exquisite lace veil which accompanied it.

But she had no intention of allowing Durstan Hayle to choose or pay for her wedding-gown. She would wear what she wished to wear, and he had no authority over her until the wedding-ring was actually on her finger.

She had no money to buy herself anything new even if she had wished to do so, but her wardrobe was in fact full of elegant gowns which she had worn in London and which had been vastly admired when she appeared in them.

She had looked them over, discarding first this one, then that, until with a smile of amusement she had chosen not a white gown, of which she had quite a number, but a green one.

She was well aware that it was the sort of unconventional action which her former acquaintances would expect, but she hoped mischievously that it would surprise and perhaps disconcert the conventional Cornish people and Durstan Hayle.

With the green gown, which was in fact meant for the evening, she had placed on her head a wide-brimmed hat which she had retrimmed with green ostrich-feathers.

It made her look very beautiful and at the same time sensational. She thought as she looked at her reflection in the mirror that Durstan Hayle would realise that she deliberately intended to appear defiant.

"I will not be subservient to him!" she told herself. "Since he has bought me, I will make his life as miserable and uncomfortable as it is possible for me to do."

Her chin went up and her green eyes gleamed as

they did when she was ready to do battle. Then as she turned away from the mirror to finish her packing she heard her father calling to her.

It was not yet time to leave for the Church and she wondered what he wanted.

She thought perhaps he had found more things he wished to take with him to Ireland.

In the ten days before her marriage Lorinda had not had a moment to herself.

Her father's excitement over going to a new country was like that of a small boy going home for the holidays.

He drank much less than usual and was intent on collecting everything in the house that he thought he might need or find attractive in the new home he intended to make for himself.

"Suppose Mr. Hayle objects to your taking these things out of the house?" Lorinda suggested. "After all, if he has bought it lock, stock, and barrel, they are really his."

"He will not want all the family portraits, and neither will you!" her father replied. "And I insist on having some of my ancestors round me."

Secretly Lorinda thought he wished to make an impression.

The Earl had already remembered quite a number of people in Ireland whom he had known over the years and had made Lorinda write letters to two or three of his former friends announcing his arrival.

Needless to say, everything he wished to take had to be packed by Lorinda and the grooms.

It was a formidable task and the small pile of personal belongings had grown to a mountain of luggage in the Hall which increased daily.

"Why not take the house with you and have done?" Lorinda asked once.

"I would if I could," the Earl replied. "If we had had Hayle's money to spend on the Priory it could have been magnificent!"

"But you would still have been living in Cornwall, Papa, which you find dull."

"That is true," he conceded. "I have always been told that Dublin is very gay and the gaming-rooms nearly as good as you can find in London."

Lorinda sighed.

There was no use warning her father against continuing to gamble. She knew it would be just a waste of words, but she could not help feeling that while he had been able to meet his debts on this occasion, another time he would not be so lucky.

"What is the point of talking about it?" she asked herself. "Papa will gamble, whatever I say or whatever the consequences."

"Lorinda!"

The Earl's voice boomed up the stairs and now she opened her bed-room door.

"Lorinda!" he shouted again.

"What is it, Papa?"

"I want you to come downstairs."

She obeyed him, moving slowly and looking as she did so at the mountain of baggage, trunks, and packing-cases which now seemed almost to fill the Hall.

The Earl would be in the Sitting-Room, she thought, but as she opened the door she found that he was not alone.

With him was Durstan Hayle.

He was looking, Lorinda had to admit to herself, extremely distinguished.

The elegance of the clothes he wore would have been outstanding in any social gathering, but as their eyes met she thought that his penetrating glance was even more unpleasant and disconcerting than she remembered it to be.

"You have to sign the marriage documents," the Earl said. "Your future husband has been obliging enough to bring them to us here so that we need not be delayed in the Vestry after the ceremony is over."

Conscious that Durstan Hayle's eyes were on her, Lorinda moved towards the desk on which reposed a number of legal parchments.

As she reached it he asked:

"You received the wedding-gown I sent you this morning?"

"It arrived," Lorinda replied.

"Then why are you not wearing it?"

"Because I prefer to be married in a gown of my own."

"What you are now wearing?"

"I hope it pleases you," she replied, knowing that it did not.

"I am superstitious."

"Can you really be so childish as to think that green is unlucky?"

"At a wedding—yes! You will please change."

"I do not intend to do so. You must take me as I am."

"I do not consider a green gown suitable for a bride, and it would certainly shock the congregation of friends and acquaintances who will be waiting for us in the Church."

"It will give them something to talk about!"

"I would consider that regrettable in the case of my wife."

Lorinda gave him a glance of sheer amusement.

"And yet you wish to marry me! I have always been talked about."

"So I understand. It is something I shall prevent happening in the future."

"I wonder," Lorinda remarked enigmatically.

She picked up the white quill pen and dipped it into the ink-pot.

"Where do you wish me to sign?" she asked.

Durstan Hayle put out his hand and laid it on the documents.

"You will change first."

She looked up at him, saw by the squareness of his chin and the hard line of his mouth that he meant what he said, and replied:

"I have already told you that I wish to be married in green."

"The woman I marry will wear white!"

They faced each other across the desk. Then with a sudden movement Durstan Hayle picked up the documents.

"I am sorry, My Lord," he said to the Earl, "but after all, these documents had best be signed in the Vestry after the marriage has taken place."

He walked towards the door.

"I will only marry a woman who looks like a bride, and I shall wait at the Church for no more than three minutes after the hour appointed for the ceremony."

He had taken both the Earl and Lorinda by surprise, and by the time they thought of anything to say he had gone.

"For God's sake, Lorinda!" her father cried. "What are you doing? Why are you behaving like this? Have you not the sense to see that he is a man with whom you cannot play fast and loose?"

Lorinda said nothing and he shouted at her:

"Go upstairs and change! Make no mistake, if we are late he will not wait. God, why did I have to have such a half-witted fool for a daughter?"

He spoke frantically and Lorinda knew it was because he was afraid that after all he would not be able to go to Ireland.

Because she knew that she could not deprive him of that pleasure and also that it was really impossible for them to stay at the Priory with no money, she went upstairs, feeling as if every footstep took her nearer to the scaffold.

How could she ever have become embroiled in such a mess? Why had she not married one of the men who had loved her in London?

Even being Ulric's mistress, she thought, would have been better than this.

But because time was passing she pulled off the green dress and old Mrs. Dogman doddled up the stairs to fasten her new white gown and to assist her in placing the lace veil on her head and securing it with a traditional wreath of orange-blossom.

When she was ready, Lorinda knew that in actual fact she looked more beautiful than she had ever done before.

The soft veil over her face gave her an ethereal beauty, as if she were one of the nymphs who according to the Cornish legends inhabited the streams and lakes.

But when she went downstairs to find her father nervously pacing up and down the Hall, his watch in his hand, she thought that her hatred of Durstan Hayle had reached new heights.

She prayed that somehow she would make him bitterly regret the manner in which he had forced her to become his wife.

"It is because he wants a Camborne," she said. "That is all I mean to him. An aristocratic name to grace his table and give him the importance to which he is not entitled by birth."

She realised as they drove towards the Church in a closed carriage which Durstan Hayle had sent from the Castle that she knew nothing at all about her future husband except that he was rich.

'He must have brains to have made money,' she thought.

But she was certain that he would be as ruthless and unpleasant in business as he had been in purchasing the Priory and herself.

"I dare say he is crooked as well!" she sneered. "A plebeian, a parvenu, who has no idea of what is right and what is wrong!"

And yet it was difficult to convince herself that Durstan Hayle was in fact of such common clay.

There was something autocratic about him which she had always associated with those of good breeding.

He at least had an eye for detail, for awaiting her at the porch was a bouquet which complemented the gown she wore.

Fashioned of lilies and gardenias, it looked very beautiful and the fragrance of it seemed for a moment to soothe some of the tempestuous violence within Lorinda's breast.

Yet, as with her hand on her father's arm she walked up the aisle and saw Durstan Hayle waiting for her, the sight of him swept away every emotion except that of hatred.

The Church was exquisitely decorated with a profusion of white flowers and every pew was filled, but not until they left the Vestry did Lorinda have a chance of seeing if there were any familiar faces amongst the congregation.

They had of course been delayed longer than was originally intended, because the marriage documents and the Deeds of the Priory had after all to be signed in the Vestry.

Lorinda also saw her father pocket an envelope which she was sure contained a cheque for forty thousand pounds.

'Durstan Hayle has made sure we cannot trick him,' she thought, and swore to herself that she would find ways of defeating him even though he fancied himself to be the conqueror.

They drove back to the Castle in an open curricule decorated with flowers and drawn by four white horses.

"Everything is for show!" Lorinda told herself contemptuously. "What he really wanted was a Circus!"

She did not look at the man sitting beside her but waved to the children who cheered as they drove through the village and the old gate-keepers who bowed and curtseyed as they entered the drive.

The Castle was looking very impressive with the sunshine glinting on the windows.

As Lorinda and her husband stepped out of the curricule the Butler welcomed them with a short address, and Lorinda saw that the other servants were lined up to greet her before they proceeded to the Banqueting-Hall.

To her surprise, they sat down fifty to the wedding-breakfast, and she found that the heads of nearly all the ancient county families had come to the wedding.

There were people who greeted her father with

pleasure, and she thought how foolish he had been not to contact his old friends when he first returned home.

It was too late now, but she fancied that if he had the choice over again he would rather have stayed in the county which was his birthplace than start a new life in a country he did not know.

Many of the guests told her they remembered her mother, but Lorinda had the feeling that they had also heard of her own exploits in London and talked to her with a slight reserve.

The food was superlative and so were the wines. Everyone appeared to be enjoying themselves, but Lorinda found it impossible to eat anything.

She was vividly conscious of the ring encircling the third finger of her left hand and the fact that Durstan Hayle had seemed to place it there with a firmness and authority which in itself was disquieting.

He had uttered his marriage vows in an uncompromising voice which made Lorinda feel that he challenged her even as they stood before the altar.

She was determined not to sound shy or let her voice falter, and when they reached the Banqueting-Hall she was equally determined to appear at her ease.

She would not let anyone, least of all her bridegroom, think that she was apprehensive or in any way intimidated by the occasion.

Because she had no wish to speak to her husband, she completely ignored him and devoted herself to the Lord Lieutenant who sat on her other side.

He was an elderly man who wished to tell her of the difficulties of the fishing industry, the expense the farmers incurred in getting their goods to markets, and a number of other local problems.

All of this, she thought vaguely, was an echo of the past which she had heard talked about ten years ago when she had last lived in Cornwall.

The meal seemed to drag on interminably, but at last the Lord Lieutenant proposed the health of the bride and groom and Durstan Hayle rose to reply.

He was brief, concise, and witty, to Lorinda's surprise, and he also appeared supremely sure of himself.

'He is so conceited,' she thought to herself scornfully, 'that it is surprising he needs my title to boost him further.'

Finally the guests said good-bye and Lorinda thought she would go to her bed-room.

"Please do not change," Durstan Hayle said to her when her foot was on the bottom step of the stairs and her hand on the bannister.

She looked at him with raised eye-brows.

"The tenants whom we shall be joining shortly will wish to see you as a bride and I would not wish you to disappoint them."

"I have no choice in the matter?" Lorinda questioned.

It was the first conversation they had had with each other since the marriage service.

"None," he answered, and walked away without waiting for her to reply.

She was shaking with rage as she went up the stairs to be met at the top by a pleasant-faced House-keeper who led her into what she had always known in the past as the Queen's Room.

It was in fact a misnomer, because the King's Room, which was occupied by the masters of the house, was where Charles I had slept, fighting the Parliamentarians.

But the local people who served in the house had thought it right that while the Master slept in the King's Room his wife should sleep in the Queen's Room.

And so Lorinda found herself in the room which had been occupied by generations of Lady Penryns.

She had last seen it with paper peeling from the walls and half the ceiling fallen on the floor, and empty of furniture.

Now she stood in the doorway, her breath taken away by the change.

The ceiling had been painted with gods and goddesses silhouetted against a celestial blue sky. Blue curtains hung over the long windows and a blue carpet covered the floor.

The bed with carved and gilded posts was draped with silk and velvet and surmounted by fronds of ostrich-feathers and was exactly the sort of bed she had always as a child imagined this room should have.

The furniture was carved and gilded and on the tables and chests were huge vases of white flowers, lilies like those in her bouquet with carnations and gardenias to scent the air.

"I hope it pleases you, M'Lady," the Housekeeper said respectfully.

"It is beautiful!" Lorinda answered. "When I remember what it used to look like, I can hardly believe that such a transformation could take place."

"The Castle is now very fine, M'Lady, and everyone who stays here says what excellent taste the Master has."

She gave a little sigh.

"But I'm thankful it's finished. We had whole armies of workmen here. Nothing's ever been done so quickly, but then, when the Master wants something, he gets it!"

That was true enough, Lorinda thought bitterly.

She took off her wreath and veil and washed her face and hands. Then the maid came to tidy her hair and replace the wreath.

There was no point, Lorinda thought, in refusing to wear the gown in which she had been married. She had fought one battle over it today and lost.

She was not inclined to challenge her husband to another duel on the same subject.

She was just ready when there came a knock at the door, and when the maid opened it her father stood outside.

"I have come to say good-bye, Lorinda."

The maid went from the room, leaving them alone, and Lorinda walked towards him.

"Your husband has done me proud and given me fast horses and out-riders to take me the first part of my journey."

"You intend to go to Bristol?"

"I shall get a ship from there which will carry me to Ireland."

"I know you are looking forward to it, Papa, and I hope it will not disappoint you."

"I have a feeling that it will be quite amusing, if nothing else," the Earl replied.

He paused, then said almost as if it was difficult to say the words:

"I shall—miss you, Lorinda."

"I hope you will, Papa."

He put his hands affectionately on her shoulders.

"Hayle will look after you. I dare say he will prove to be quite an amenable husband, even if at the moment he does behave as if he were God Almighty!"

Lorinda laughed. She could not help it.

"That is exactly what he thinks he is, Papa!"

Her father smiled at her.

"Well, I dare say you will cut him down to size. Every man you ever met has ended up a slave, one way or another, and I do not suppose that Hayle will be the exception."

"I hope not," Lorinda answered.

She did not however feel very optimistic at the moment about enslaving Durstan Hayle.

He seemed to be completely impervious to her charms, and there was something unbending about him which she had never found before in any other man.

Then she told herself she was being unduly apprehensive.

None of the Beaux and Bucks who had pursued her in London had ever been anything but abjectly servile after they had known her a little while.

It might have been her indifference, it might have been because she was always out of their reach; but

whatever the reason, sooner or later they had suc-
cumbed to being humble, grateful for the smallest
favour she might extend to them, and willing to obey
her every command.

Lorinda looked at her father and smiled.

"Do not worry about me, Papa. I shall manage all
right."

"I hope so," the Earl said in all sincerity. Then he
added: "If the worst comes to the worst you can always run away. I will write and tell you what Ireland
is like. We might be together again after all."

Lorinda thought that once again he was cheating
but she did not say so.

"I shall remember that, Papa," she said aloud and
kissed his cheek.

He held her close to him for a moment, then he released her and looked round the bed-room.

"At least you will not have to worry where the next
meal is coming from!"

"Nor will you!" Lorinda retorted. "But be careful,
Papa. The next time you are in the red there may
not be a wealthy Nabob from India ready to ante-
up!"

The gambling slang made her father laugh. Then
he had gone and although Lorinda told herself it was
ridiculous she felt suddenly very alone.

It was the largeness of the house, she tried to tell
herself, but she knew there was only one reason why
she felt apprehensive.

It was because she was now to all intents and pur-
poses alone with her husband.

* * *

The tenants' party in the great barn had reached
the noisy stage.

Huge barrels of ale and the Cornish cider which
was most intoxciating had already been circulating
for some hours when Lorinda and her husband arrived.

They were greeted with cheers as everyone rose to
their feet, some a trifle unsteadily, and were led by

the Agent to two chairs which seemed almost like thrones at the end of the room.

There were speeches from several of the leading farmers and Durstan Hayle spoke again.

This time he was even more amusing, so much so that he had his audience roaring with laughter and, perhaps more acceptably, he promised them all six months free of rent in commemoration of his marriage.

This news was received with tumultuous applause.

As they went round shaking hands with their guests, Lorinda could not help feeling that Durstan Hayle had established himself not only as a Landlord but also as a very important personage in this his particular world, and she was in fact of little consequence.

The women, however, wished her good luck and some of them shyly gave her pieces of white heather and little shells which Lorinda felt uncomfortably were fertility charms.

Afterwards they all went outside to watch a display of fireworks, with rockets storming up into the darkening sky and showers of gold and silver rain exploding against the shadowy bushes.

Lorinda began to feel tired and when at last Durstan Hayle said they could withdraw she moved thankfully into a large Salon which she had not seen before.

It was a very beautiful room, but she was too weary to admire the pictures or the furniture, and glancing at the clock she saw that it was half past ten.

It was not very late by London standards but she had been giving a nonstop performance, she thought, since noon.

"Let me offer you a drink?" Durstan Hayle suggested.

"No, thank you."

"May I say that you have come through what must have been a considerable ordeal with flying colours?"

Lorinda was surprised that he should compliment her.

She had had an uncomfortable feeling all day that he was being critical about everything she said and did.

"Tomorrow I have quite a number of wedding presents to show you," he went on. "There was no reason to have them on display and my secretary has arranged them in one of the Drawing-Rooms for your inspection."

"There were none for me, I suppose?"

He did not reply and after a moment she asked:

"Did you put a notice of our marriage in *The Gazette?*"

"No."

She raised her eye-brows.

"Why not?"

"I thought it might seem strange that you should marry so quickly after leaving London. There could only be one ostensible reason for the speed."

"You mean because you are rich?"

"Exactly!"

"It would be difficult for you to have to explain that the real reason was that you wanted a wife with adjoining lands and a title?"

Lorinda meant to be unpleasant but her husband ignored her jibe.

"I expect you wish to retire," he remarked.

She felt irritated because he had suggested it first. She rose to her feet.

"I am indeed fatigued," she said, "and shaking hands with so many people is exhausting."

They walked together to the foot of the stairs where there was a footman on duty.

Lorinda wanted to say good-night in a voice that would make it clear that she did not expect to see Durstan Hayle again before morning, but she was afraid that this might incite him to the very action she wished to avoid.

Without looking back at him she moved slowly up the staircase.

She wondered if he was watching her but would not turn her head to find out.

As she entered her bed-room to find the maids waiting, she thought that her heart was beating in an unaccountable manner.

Only when finally she was left alone did she acknowledge to herself that she was frightened.

The mere idea of Durstan Hayle even touching her, much less making her his wife, was more frightening than anything she had ever imagined.

She hated him and she thought to be touched by him would be a worse hell than anything that a preacher could envisage.

"I loathe him!" she told herself.

As the maids left the room she ran to the door to turn the key in the lock, then stared at it incredulously.

There was no key!

She had never for a moment anticipated that any house which had everything including locks which were embossed and gilded should not possess a key.

She opened the door to see if by any chance the key was outside, thinking perhaps that the rooms were locked when they were unoccupied. There was no key!

She inspected the communicating-room which led to a Sitting-Room but there was no key there either, and she stood thinking for a moment, realising that something like panic was rising within her.

Then with an effort she fought back her feelings and knew that she would fight him with her very last breath, fight him so that while she might be his wife in name she would never, if she was conscious, be his in any other way.

She sped across the room and pulled open the drawers of an inlaid chest.

She had put what she sought amongst her luggage, which she had packed before she had left home, and there in the same drawer as her gloves and handkerchiefs she found it—the pistol she always carried to protect herself against Highwaymen and Footpads.

It was in a box which also contained bullets and she loaded it. The cold steel against her fingers gave her a sense of security.

"If I use it I must not shoot to kill," she told herself. "I will just wing him in the arm, and that will prevent him from making a nuisance of himself for some time."

Lorinda was, as it happened, an extremely good shot.

Because she had always known how deeply her father resented her not being a boy she had made herself proficient in all sports which would have been the prerogative of her brother, if she had had one.

Ever since she was old enough to sit on a horse she had ridden astride. She could shoot game birds as well as any man could, and she had practised with a revolver until it was very rare for her to miss the bull's-eye of any target.

Before she left Cornwall when she was ten she would race not her contemporaries but the stable-lads over the jumps that were used for steeple-chases.

She rode the same horses they did, helped to school them even at that early age, and had such a good seat and hands that the old groom would say:

"Ye were born with 'em, M'Lady. That's something Oi can't teach."

With her pistol in her hand Lorinda sat down in a chair which faced the door.

Her maids had helped her into a diaphanous lace-trimmed nightgown which she had brought from London, but she put over it not the negligée which matched, but a rest-gown of quilted satin that was warm and certainly less revealing.

Now Lorinda tied the sash tightly round her waist and hoped that her beauty would not make her husband lose his head, which was the effect it had had on so many other men.

Always, sooner or later when she was with a man, he lost control of himself and tried to clasp her to him and kiss her.

Lorinda had had to fight off a number of ardent suitors from time to time, but none of them had been able to hold her for more than a few seconds and she had never yet been kissed.

The mere idea made her feel sick and angry to the point where she had often thought that if they went much further she would in fact commit murder!

"I will handle Durstan as I handled the others," Lorinda told herself.

Then unaccountably she remembered the man who had held her in an iron grip when she wished to join the smugglers.

She had been so busy these past two weeks that she had almost forgotten her humiliating experience, or the manner in which some stranger had smothered her mouth with his hand and lifted her off her feet with an arm of steel.

"He attacked me from behind," she excused herself. "Durstan and I will meet face to face."

She sat watching the door, her loaded pistol tucked down beside her just within reach of her right hand.

When he did come she would show him in this instance if none other that she intended to be master.

* * *

Lorinda awoke with a jerk.

For a moment she could not think where she was, then she realised that the candles were gutted low and she was sitting in an armchair, feeling cold and stiff.

He had not come!

Her pistol was still beside her but no-one had opened the door.

Rising to her feet, shivering, she looked at the Dresden china clock on the mantelpiece and saw that the hands were pointing at three o'clock.

She stared at it incredulously. She must have slept for at least three hours!

One thing was certain, her husband would not visit her now and she could get into bed.

She took off her satin wrap, looking at the door apprehensively as she did so in case he should choose this moment to appear.

She slipped between the sheets and just as a precaution she put her loaded pistol under the pillow beside her.

The bed was warm and comfortable but she did not fall asleep immediately as she had expected. Instead, she found herself wondering why she had been left alone.

Somehow it seemed unlikely that he should not insist on his rights.

Then an incredible thought struck her. Was it possible—could the reason be that he did not find her attractive?

Lorinda could hardly credit that this could be the truth.

Yet if she was honest with herself she had to admit that ever since she had known Durstan Hayle he had never looked at her in a manner that she could possibly construe as showing admiration.

Even today when she had worn the wedding-gown he had chosen for her and the veil he had provided, she had thought the few times she looked at him that there was a mocking expression in his eyes and a contemptuous curl to his lips, which irritated her profoundly.

Was it possible—was it really credible that of all the men in the world she might have married she had found the one who was not the least interested in her as a woman?

It was such a revolutionary idea that for a moment Lorinda thought she must be mistaken.

Then, even while she was relieved at the thought that she would not have to fight to keep her husband from touching her, at the same time something feminine in her was outraged by his indifference.

There was such a long line of conquests behind her and she had grown so used to the adulation and the compliments of everyone she knew, except for the older generation, that Lorinda was stunned and startled by this departure from everything that was familiar.

Then with a sudden sinking of her spirits and a despondency she could not suppress she found herself asking a question.

If he was not attracted to her, how then had she any chance of mastering him and getting her own way?

It was dawn before Lorinda fell asleep, and when she awoke it was to find that the problem which had beset her last night was still in her mind.

The maids called her as she had told them to do at eight o'clock and because she had no wish to encounter her husband earlier in the day than she must she asked for her breakfast in bed.

It was brought to her elegantly served on a tray covered with a lace cloth, the dishes of crested silver, the plates and cup of the best Sèvres china.

Lorinda could not help remembering the breakfasts which had been slapped on the table at the Priory by Mrs. Dogman and the chipped china and tarnished silver she and her father had been forced to use.

"Will you enquire what plans have been made for the morning?" she asked one of the maids.

"The Master asked me to tell you when you were awake, M'Lady, that he'll be riding at a half after ten o'clock and would wish you to accompany him."

"Thank you," Lorinda said aloud. "Will you please have my riding-habit ready?"

But to herself she thought resentfully that it was another command.

There was no question of whether she would like to join him, merely that he wished her to do so.

'We shall have to come to an understanding over this sooner or later,' she thought.

She had an instinctive feeling that it might be a very difficult thing to do.

As she rose to step into the bath that had been

prepared for her, she suddenly thought to herself that if she was to gain her own way, if she was to get her husband as enslaved as other men had been, then the first thing she must do was captivate him.

She drew in her breath at the thought and knew that her first instinct was to go on fighting, pitting her will against his, defying him at every turn, making his life such a purgatory that eventually he would be forced to give in to her.

Then she had the uncomfortable feeling that such tactics would never achieve the desired result and that if it came to a battle of wills he would emerge the victor.

No, she would have to be more subtle than that.

She must be charming, she must make it impossible for him not to become enslaved by her beauty as every other man had been.

It would not be easy, she thought, to hide her dislike, but somehow she would manage it.

As in everything else in life she had ever wanted, she would work towards a certain goal and achieve her objective by sheer persistence.

"I will make him love me," Lorinda told herself. "Then he will suffer as he deserves to suffer for the way he has behaved."

She brushed aside the knowledge that he had saved her father from a great deal of misery, and that he had paid far more than was necessary for the Priory and for the doubtful privilege of marrying her.

She hated him so vehemently that she was determined to conquer him by any means, fair or foul.

"He shall love me," she told herself grimly, "and when he does I will laugh at him as I have laughed at so many other men."

She knew that laughter was a far more subtle weapon than cold steel, especially where a man's emotions were concerned.

She remembered how she had often laughed at Edward as she spurned him, and yet he had always come back like a faithful dog, begging for more.

That was the way she would punish Durstan Hayle for daring to force her into becoming his wife.

That was the way she would have her revenge. That was how she would be the victor, whatever the odds against her.

And of one thing she would make quite certain— that she did not have to sit every night waiting apprehensively with a pistol in her hand for a husband who was not interested in her.

Casually she said to the maid:

"I see there is no key in the lock. Sometimes I lock my door if I wish to rest undisturbed in the afternoon. Will you ask the Housekeeper to find out what has happened to it?"

"Yes, of course, M'Lady," the maid said. "I can't imagine why it has disappeared."

It was in fact a mystery, Lorinda thought, because there seemed to be no reason for Durstan Hayle to take the key if he did not intend to use the opportunity an open door to her bed-room gave him.

Dressed in a thin green habit which echoed her eyes and was frogged with white braid, Lorinda looked very alluring.

The tricorn hat she wore had a green feather which curled over one ear and had caused a sensation in Hyde Park the first time she had worn it.

She took a great deal of extra trouble in arranging her hair, and her riding-boots beneath her full skirt were polished until they shone like mirrors as she walked down the stairs.

Her silver spurs clinked, her stiff petticoats rustled, and she thought to herself she was the perfect combination of soft, feminine woman and militant man!

She forced a gentleness to her eyes which she did not feel and her lips were red and inviting as she saw Durstan Hayle in the Hall and smiled at him beguilingly.

"I accept your invitation to go riding with the greatest of pleasure," she said. "Have you any particular destination in mind?"

"I thought you might like to see some of the improvements which I have made to the farms," he said, "such as I now wish to carry out on the Priory Estate."

"That will be delightful," Lorinda replied with a soft note in her voice.

If he was surprised at the change in the manner in which she spoke to him he did not show it.

Instead they walked side by side towards the front door and only when she looked at the horses outside did Lorinda have no need to pretend an enthusiasm and excitement—she actually felt it.

Never before had she seen more magnificent examples of horse-flesh.

The mare she was to ride was coal-black except for a white star on her nose and one white fetlock.

The stallion which was Durstan Hayle's was also black but without a mark of any kind on his smooth, shining coat.

Lorinda went to the head of the mare, patting her nose, talking to her in a gentle voice as one might talk to a child.

"What is her name?" she asked.

"Ayshea," Durstan Hayle replied. "I have given all my horses Indian names and the stallion I am riding is called Akbar."

The groom helped Lorinda into the saddle.

She felt Ayshea respond to her touch on the reins, and knew the same feeling of pleasure and power a musician feels when he evokes music from a superb instrument.

For the first time in weeks, she forgot everything but the joy of riding an animal the equal of which she had never before known.

For a moment her hatred was suspended and she was happy with a happiness that seemed to be part of the sunshine.

CHAPTER FIVE

Resting before dinner, Lorinda thought that the day had been unsatisfactory in that her efforts to charm her husband had been singularly unprogressive.

He had been polite and courteous, and had, she thought, by nature extremely good manners.

But while he talked to her on quite interesting subjects, she might have been his maiden aunt for all the impact she appeared to have made on him.

Never at any time did she see an admiring glint in his eyes, which she knew was essential to her self-esteem.

Always in the past men had looked at her at first in astonishment, overwhelmed by her beauty, then with an obvious desire to make her their own, to touch her, to possess her in some way.

Once they were captivated there had been for them no escape.

But not for one second when she was with Durstan Hayle did he seem to treat her as an attractive woman or even, for that matter, as a woman at all.

She tried some of the wiles she had seen used in the past, which although she had never needed herself she had noticed in other women were singularly effective.

She asked him questions with a wide-eyed innocence which made all men feel superior.

He answered them interestingly and positively, then usually let the subject drop, so that it was up to Lorinda to find another topic of conversation.

He talked with some enthusiasm of the improvements he was making on the Estate and she found in fact that he was using all the advanced methods of farming, most of which she was honest enough to admit she had never heard of before.

He was also putting some acres into the cultivation of flowers, especially spring daffodils and tulips, which he thought might have a sale in the larger city markets if only they could convey them there quickly enough.

He was inventing a special lightly sprung vehicle which, pulled by a team of four horses, would be able to reach Plymouth, Bath, and perhaps Bristol in a far quicker time than had ever been achieved before.

Lorinda found herself more interested than she had expected to be, and after a while her questions became more intelligent and she forgot that she was trying to pretend that she was a helpless feminine woman.

They had had luncheon at a farm-house on the very border of the Estate.

Only as they rode home did Lorinda realise that while she had actually enjoyed herself, her ambition to make Durstan Hayle aware of her was as far from being realised as it had been when they had set out that morning.

"I am surprised you have not married before," she said provocatively as they slowed their horses over a piece of rough ground on which it would be dangerous to gallop.

"I have been living in the East," he replied. "It is not really a suitable climate for Englishwomen."

"I cannot believe that you were without female companionship."

He smiled.

"That is a very different matter."

"Are they very alluring, the Indian women who look upon men as supreme beings?"

"Very!" he answered briefly.

Lorinda felt herself stiffen.

It was just what he would like, she thought savagely, a woman who would kow-tow to him and obey his slightest wish.

"But you are glad to be back in England?" she persisted. "Even though you had to leave your alluring dark-eyed houri behind you?"

He did not answer and she had the feeling that he thought her remark in bad taste.

He did not say so, but she felt instinctively that he disapproved of a lady speaking of such matters of which she should know nothing.

'He expects me to be nothing but a cipher—a puppet without any brains! He might as well have married the figure-head of a ship!' Lorinda thought angrily.

Because once again she was hating him they rode on in silence.

When they reached the Castle, Durstan Hayle said as he dismounted:

"I have some work to do which will take me until dinner-time. I expect you wish to rest."

"How kind of you to consider my wishes," Lorinda replied sarcastically.

She swept up the stairs and into her bed-room, feeling that once again he had defeated her and that he was as inflexible and unbending as a wall of steel.

She had been followed into her bed-room by one of the two Dalmatian hounds which Durstan Hayle owned. Caesar and Brutus were in their own way as highly bred and as faultless as their Master's horses.

Because she suddenly felt the need for consolation, Lorinda pulled off her hat, threw it onto a chair, and sitting down on the floor pulled Caesar into her arms.

He was delighted with the attention he was receiving and she sat caressing him for a long time, feeling that his affection was some compensation for the coldness she received from his owner.

Then when Lorinda undressed herself he lay beside her, keeping a watchful eye on her in a manner that was comforting.

When she had her bath the maid asked her which of her gowns she would wear that evening.

The woman opened the wardrobe and Lorinda looked for the first time with interest at the vast array of clothes which Durstan Hayle had ordered from London.

If it had been any other man she would have appreciated his eye for detail in that he had gone to a shop from which she had occasionally been able to afford one expensive gown and had ordered wholesale.

The dressmaker, a Madame Rachelle, who had come from Paris, had known Lorinda's size in shoes and there were slippers to match every gown.

She also found a profusion of silk and lace underwear such as she had often dreamt of owning.

But perversity made her choose one of the gowns that she had brought with her from the Priory, and because she wanted to see Durstan Hayle's reaction to it she chose one that was so daring that she had in fact never worn it.

She had bought it on an impulse when all her friends wished to be alluring to the point where they bared their breasts or else covered them merely with the finest flesh-coloured gauze.

The gown Lorinda chose was a very pale yellow, in such a fine material that she looked naked from the waist up.

The décolletage was outrageously low, and so was the back, and the fragile material lined with flesh-colour barely concealed the rosy tips of her breasts.

She looked in the mirror when she was ready to go downstairs and thought that she was glad that only her husband would see her.

At the same time, she was extremely interested to see what his reaction would be.

She was well aware that her appearance would excite any other man she knew to madness.

She could envisage with very little difficulty what Lord Wroxford would feel, and it would certainly have sent Edward Hinton into a state of drooling imbecility.

The maid dressed her flaming red hair to a fullness which made her pointed face seem smaller and very poignant.

Her green eyes were enormous and her lips artificially redder than usual as she walked down the stairs.

As she had expected, Durstan Hayle was waiting for her in the Salon.

She made her entrance as dramatically as possible, standing still for a moment in the doorway, then advancing towards him very slowly so that he could see the full effect of her gown.

She knew that the lighted chandeliers above their heads would illuminate every detail of her exquisite figure and her eyes were on his face as she searched for his response.

He waited until she reached his side, then he said:

"I ordered some gowns for you from London. I cannot believe that this monstrosity was included amongst them."

"You do not like it?" Lorinda asked in sweet surprise. "I imagined it would please you."

"It is the sort of gown I would expect a droxy to wear—not my wife!"

"Are you not being very old-fashioned?"

"You will change immediately into something more respectable."

"It is too late, and I have no wish to change."

"I order you to do so!"

"I have no intention of obeying such an order, nor do I acknowledge your right to give it!"

Lorinda faced him defiantly, her eyes looking into his, and she knew as they faced each other that once again it was a duel of wills.

"Very well," Durstan Hayle said at last. "If you wish to be naked why not be realistic about it?"

He put out his hand as he spoke, and taking hold of the soft material in the centre of Lorinda's bodice, with one swift movement he tore it down to her waist.

She gave a cry of astonishment and instinctively put her hands over her naked breasts.

She saw the triumph in his expression, then turned and fled.

Only as she reached the door did his voice, hard and uncompromising, check her.

"I am expecting you to dine with me," he said, "and I will give you five minutes to change, after which I shall come and fetch you!"

She did not reply or look back.

She only ran across the Hall, holding the tattered remnants of her gown across her breasts in some effort at modesty.

When she reached the sanctity of her bed-room, her maid was there tidying the room.

"What's happened, M'Lady?" she asked in consternation.

"There has been an accident," Lorinda was forced to explain.

The maid helped her into another gown, one of those which had come from London, and it was in fact a very attractive garment.

She did not even look at herself in the mirror, she merely let the maid dress her as if she were a doll, and was acutely conscious of the clock ticking on the mantelpiece.

If Durstan Hayle had said he would come and fetch her, she knew he would keep his word, and she had been humiliated enough without being involved in a scene which would start the servants talking.

When she was ready her maid asked:

"Shall I have this gown mended for you, M'Lady?"

"Throw it away!" Lorinda replied sharply. "I never wish to see it again!"

As she walked down the stairs Durstan Hayle came from the Salon and she knew that dinner was served.

He made no comment about her appearance but merely offered her his arm, and, hating to touch him, loathing his very proximity, she walked silently beside him towards the Dining-Room.

* * *

Surprisingly, Lorinda slept dreamlessly, only to wake feeling that she was involved in a nightmare which might go on indefinitely.

"How can we live like this?" she asked herself.

For the first time the idea of battling interminably with a man who always won filled her with apprehension and dismay.

She was honest enough to know that she had deliberately provoked him last night and yet his reaction had been unexpected.

She had thought he might be angry, but his violence had upset her to the point where she now admitted to herself that she was a little afraid of him.

"It is only because he is unpredictable," she said. "Any other man would have reacted quite differently, but with him I never know what to expect."

After her breakfast had been brought to her she asked a little apprehensively what were the plans for today.

"The Master is expecting you to ride with him again this morning, M'Lady," the maid answered. "He has ordered the mare you rode yesterday."

That at least was a relief, Lorinda thought.

When she was riding Ayshea she could forget her hatred of the man who rode beside her and concentrate instead on the sheer delight of being mounted on such a magnificent animal.

At the same time, she suspected that Ayshea was one of his favourite horses and she did not at the moment feel kindly to any favourite of his.

She chose a riding-habit in golden yellow which was even more becoming than the one she had worn the day before.

"I do not suppose he will notice," she murmured to herself.

"Did you speak, M'Lady?" the maid asked.

"Only to myself," Lorinda replied.

Her hat had been made for her by one of the most important Milliners in London.

She remembered a dozen men who had exclaimed at her appearance when she had first worn it, and she had known by the expression in their eyes that it made her look more than usually desirable.

Only a man with a heart of stone would be able to resist her.

Then she wondered if Durstan Hayle was only attracted by women who were dark-haired and doe-eyed with a sensuous, lissom grace which no Westerner, however graceful, could emulate.

"I should be grateful that he does not desire to touch me," she told herself.

Yet she could not pretend that it did not irritate her that he was apparently impervious to her attractions.

She went downstairs to find that her husband was not as she expected waiting for her in the Hall.

"The Master's in the Library, M'Lady," the Butler informed her.

Lorinda was just about to join him there when he came from the room accompanied by his secretary and the Agent.

He finished his instructions to them, then turned to her.

"My apologies, Lorinda," he said, "but I am afraid after all I cannot accompany you this morning. I have to go to Falmouth on some urgent business."

Lorinda did not speak but looked through the open front door to where the horses were waiting.

"You will not however miss your ride," he went on. "A groom will accompany you."

"There is no need for that," Lorinda said. "I much prefer to ride alone."

"A groom will go with you!" he said briefly.

She glared at him angrily.

"I have already told you that I have no wish for one. I always ride alone."

He walked across the Hall and opened the door into the Salon.

"Will you come in here a moment?" he asked.

She obeyed him, wondering what he had to say.

He shut the door behind him.

"Let me make this quite clear, Lorinda," he said in an uncompromising voice. "It is conventional and correct for a lady when she rides to be accompanied by a groom, and I wish my wife to be both these things."

"It is quite ridiculous!" Lorinda retorted. "Who is to see me?"

"That is not the point."

"I will not be followed by a servant who will doubtless run tittle-tattling to you if I do anything in the least unconventional!"

"I will order a groom to go with you and I do not intend to discuss the matter any further!"

Durstan Hayle opened the door and went back into the Hall. Lorinda heard him give instructions that Akbar be taken back to the stables and that a groom on a different horse should come round immediately.

She stood listening and biting her lower lip as she did so.

It infuriated her that her wishes should be overruled in such a high-handed manner. She positively disliked the idea of being accompanied by a servant.

She had always ridden alone even when she was a child, and in London she had never bothered to take a groom with her when she rode in Hyde Park.

Granted, the moment she appeared there were a number of adoring young men awaiting her arrival, so that she was encompassed by a cavalcade as she trotted in the Row.

When they were in the more unfashionable part of the Park, Lorinda had always put her horse into a gallop.

Sometimes she had even gone further afield on her own, riding to Hampstead Heath or even to the fields which lay beyond Chelsea.

But now she must be nannied and chaperoned as if she were a child or one of the Society women who she had always said disparagingly could "only ride a rocking-horse."

It was an insult to her pride.

But because she felt to argue further might mean that her husband would forbid her to ride at all, she waited, tapping her foot impatiently, for the groom's appearance.

While she was doing so, the Phaeton, which she had admired the first time Durstan Hayle had called on her father, came to the front door.

If he remembered that she was standing in the Salon he gave no sign of it. He merely stepped into the Phaeton, picked up the reins, and drove off.

Lorinda moved across the Hall to watch him.

There was no doubt he could drive with an expertise that was outstanding and there was something very elegant and at the same time dashing about the squareness of his shoulders and the angle at which he wore his top-hat.

"He may *look* like that," she told herself scornfully, "but at heart he is just a fuddy-duddy, old-fashioned, out-of-date, and as sanctimonious as a Church Service!"

She hated him anew as he disappeared up the drive in a cloud of dust.

Then she saw the groom coming hurriedly from the stables, riding a frisky roan which he was having some trouble controlling.

She was helped onto Ayshea's side-saddle and put her right leg over the pommel. Then she led the way out of the court-yard, aware that the groom was riding the conventional length behind her.

Already her brain was making a plan, concocting a way to circumvent her husband's orders.

She deliberately rode north and soon they were clear of the Park and the village and were out in wild open country where the grass was thick with wild flowers.

It was then that Lorinda pushed Ayshea into a gallop, and she settled down to ride with all the skill that had made her an outstanding horse-woman.

The roan on which the groom was mounted was fresh and he kept just behind her for at least a mile.

Then glancing back over her shoulder Lorinda realised she was beginning to draw ahead of him.

She was well aware that while the roan was an excellent animal, it would not have the stamina of Ayshea, nor was the groom likely to equal her horsemanship.

On and on she galloped, but looking back saw him still in sight behind her and knew he was determined that she should not get away from him.

Suddenly she felt that the groom was a symbol of everything that she disliked about Durstan Hayle—his censorious attitude towards her, his desire for respectability, and most of all the fact that he did not look upon her as an attractive woman.

To evade the groom who was there on his orders would be a positive blow against the man she hated, a defiant gesture which would teach him she was not the slave he wanted her to be.

For the first time she applied her whip to Ayshea and used her spur.

The mare leapt forward under this hitherto unused stimulation.

Now with her lips set in a hard line, her eyes sparkling with anger, Lorinda continued to drive the spur home.

She was driven by a frenzy that was quite uncontrollable; a revolt against everything she had suffered at her husband's hands since the first moment she had met him.

She was carrying a long flexible whip and she began to lash Ayshea with it, keeping the mare at full gallop as she alternately whipped and spurred her.

There was nothing reasonable about her action, it came from an emotional explosion which shook her to the depths of her being.

She knew she was being cruel but the mastery over her husband's favourite, Ayshea, as she outstripped the groom, gave her a strange exhilaration.

It was as if Durstan was pursuing her, striving to capture her, determined that she should not escape from the trap in which he had caught her.

Again and again she dug in her pointed spur and whipped Ayshea to make her go faster. Only speed could take her out of reach of the man she hated!

They must have galloped for miles when suddenly, without any warning, the mare caught her foot in a rabbit-hole.

She staggered, fell forward on her knees, and shot Lorinda over her head.

The ground was not hard and although Lorinda was jarred by the fall she was not knocked unconscious but only breathless.

She lay for a moment and felt that the mad, impetuous impulse which had run through her veins like fire had left her and that she had in fact been jolted back to her senses.

She sat up and straightened her hat, and as she did so she looked at the mare.

She saw first that Ayshea was lame, then noticed the weals on her off quarter and the blood on her near flank.

The sight made Lorinda draw in her breath.

Never in her whole life had she used a spur on a trained animal but only on one she was breaking in. Never had she been cruel enough to draw blood or inflict suffering on a horse that was doing what she required of it.

Unsteadily she rose to her feet.

"Oh . . . Ayshea . . . I am sorry!" she said. "Forgive me! Oh, my dear . . . forgive me!"

She put out her hands to soothe the frightened animal, patting her neck, talking to the mare softly until she nuzzled her nose confidently against Lorinda as if in forgiveness.

"How could I have behaved like that?" Lorinda asked herself, aghast.

She had always loathed cruelty in every form.

Yet because of what she had suffered from her husband, she had made his favourite, Ayshea, pay to the point of brutality when the mare had done nothing to deserve it.

She hid her face against Ayshea's mane and fought

back the tears that seemed likely to choke her. Then
she turned the mare round, realising as she did so
that she was in fact very lame.

It meant that they would have to walk home slowly,
and they started back over the rough ground over
which no horseman with any sense would have galloped.

It was going to take hours, she knew, to walk back
the miles they had come.

She thought to herself that it was a fittingly humiliating punishment for the manner in which she had behaved.

Trying to find the easiest path for Ayshea, Lorinda
found herself whispering again and again:

"I am sorry! Oh, my dear . . . I am so . . . sorry!" and
she felt somehow that the horse understood.

It was more than four hours later that she saw the
Castle in the distance.

She had hoped that they might encounter the
groom, who would still be looking for her.

But in her desire to give him the slip, she had
twisted and turned and it would have been quite easy
for him to lose the direction in which she had gone.

It would take her about another hour, she knew, to
reach the Castle, and by now she was very tired and
was finding it increasingly hard to walk in riding-boots.

There was nothing she could do but plod on, encouraging the lame horse and knowing the sooner Ayshea was in her own stable and in the capable hands
of the Head-groom, the better.

It was afternoon before they reached the drive leading to the Castle.

They must have been seen in the distance by the
grooms, who were obviously watching out for them,
for when they were halfway towards the house the
men came running.

Lorinda knew by the expressions in their eyes that
the groom who had accompanied her had already returned home with an account of her behaviour.

"Ayshea is not only lame," she said to the Head-
groom, "but her flank needs poulticing."

She did not wait to see the expression of consternation on his face, but walked away, leaving the mare to be attended to, and entering the house went straight upstairs.

A maid helped her to take off her riding-habit and pulled off her high-necked riding-boots, dusty from walking, with the spur covered in blood.

The skirt of her riding-habit was stained too and Lorinda averted her eyes from it.

"Leave everything now," she said to the maid. "You can tidy later, I want to be alone."

"Very good, M'Lady."

The maid put the riding-boots down by the dressing-table and left Lorinda's whip, hat, and riding-gloves on a chair.

Lorinda put on a thin negligé and sank down on the couch in front of the windows and stretched herself on the soft cushions.

The maid covered her with a light rug of satin and lace and withdrew from the room.

Lorinda closed her eyes.

She was appalled by her behaviour and by her lack of self-control.

How could she have lamed Ayshea and inflicted such punishment on her when the person she really wanted to hurt was her husband?

She was ashamed and she also felt terribly depressed. How could she degrade herself in behaving like a savage?

She must have been resting for nearly an hour and was in fact half-asleep when suddenly the door opened and without a knock or any preliminaries Durstan Hayle came into the room.

It was the first time he had been to her bed-room and because she was so surprised to see him there Lorinda sat up on the couch.

She looked at him. Then felt as if her heart had stopped beating.

Never in her whole life had she seen a man so angry.

His face was contorted with rage, and while she had

always thought of him as cold and hard, now his expression was so changed that he appeared to her as violent and ferocious as the devil!

He advanced a little way into the room, then he said:

"I have just seen Ayshea. What explanation have you for such barbaric behaviour?"

There was a note in his voice, although he did not raise it, which made Lorinda instinctively rise to her feet.

She had been ready to apologise for injuring the horse, even though she told herself that Durstan Hayle had driven her to it.

But now her hatred of him flared up afresh and she felt as she had when she had galloped away from the groom, that she must escape from the subservience he was forcing upon her.

He came a little nearer and she thought that the fury in his eyes gave him an expression she had never seen before. She could hardly believe it was the same man she had married.

"I was aware that you were completely insensitive to the feelings of other people," he said. "I knew you were selfish, spoilt, and callous in a manner that no woman should be, but I did not believe you were capable of such cruelty as you have inflicted on one of my favourite mares!"

He paused. Then he said slowly, in a manner that made it all the more ominous:

"In the circumstances it is only right and just that you should receive the same treatment!"

Lorinda did not understand.

Then she gave a little gasp as she saw that Durstan Hayle picked up from the chair her own riding-whip which she had used so cruelly on Ayshea.

It flashed through her mind that this could not be happening to her and was but a figment of her imagination.

Then with a swift movement that made her cry out in sheer terror Durstan Hayle twisted her round and flung her onto the couch.

Her face landed in the softness of a satin cushion and as she turned her head in an effort to breathe she felt the whip strike her across the back.

The agony of it seemed to sear its way from her body into her mind.

Three times he struck her, then as she felt the pain was almost intolerable he threw down the whip and took hold of her arm.

"None of my horses has ever before had to be poulticed," he said in that hard voice that terrorised her. "I imagine you do not know what a spur feels like, so you had best learn!"

He picked up her left riding-boot, which the maid had left beside the dressing-table, and pushed back the soft sleeve of her wrap. Then incredibly, unbelievably, into the soft part of her shoulder Lorinda felt the sharp prick of a spur!

She screamed before she could prevent herself.

Then with an iron resolution that came from a pride which managed to surmount the pain, she endured without a sound the two other pricks that he gave her.

She heard him throw the boot down onto the carpet beside the whip before his footsteps crossed the room and the door slammed behind him.

She lay as he left her, unable to move, finding it difficult for the moment to breathe.

She could not believe this had happened to her.

She, the most acclaimed and beautiful woman in London, who had never allowed a man to touch her in love, had been whipped and spurred like a horse.

Her back was throbbing intolerably, but far worse than the physical agony was the humiliation within herself.

Like most women, Lorinda had never encountered violence, except from a man wishing to take her into his arms.

The violence which she had encountered now and the superior strength of a man against whom she had no defence was something which struck deep into her very soul.

She was past hatred; past any feeling at the moment except for a wish to die—to escape from the unknown future, from something so ominous and so overpowering that she could not even define it.

"What . . . shall I . . . do? How can I . . . bear this?" she asked herself.

Still without moving, she contemplated running away, feeling that after what he had done to her it would be impossible for her ever to face her husband again.

How could she look at him, knowing the way he had treated her?

How could she encounter the mocking expression in his eyes and the twist of his lips, knowing that he was gloating over the manner in which he had humiliated her and sneering at her helplessness.

In that moment Lorinda went down into a hell so deep and so dark that she thought it must extinguish her.

Then the pride which had always been one of her virtues and the courage she had never lacked came to her rescue.

Slowly she came back from sheer agonised feeling to constructive thought.

He had humbled her deeper than she had believed any man could humble a woman, treating her as cruelly as if she were an animal, but she would not give him the satisfaction of realising it.

She would not be defeated, she would not be subservient, whatever he might do to her!

Slowly, conscious of how much it hurt her, Lorinda rose from the couch.

She did not need to see her back to know that the whip would have left three great weals on her white skin, which had been given no protection by the diaphanous material of her wrap.

It was easy, however, to see the three spur-marks on her shoulder. Each had drawn blood and now were beginning to swell.

She walked to the dressing-table to sit down on the stool in front of the mirror and stare at her reflection.

She thought after all she had been through she

would look different. Instead, although she was very pale, she was in fact as beautiful as she had ever been.

She had a mad impulse to slash her face with a knife and make herself so ugly that Durstan Hayle would have to go through life accompanied by a wife who was so hideous that people would look away when they saw her.

Then she told herself that to show him she was in any way upset by his action would be just what he wanted.

He had surprised her—very well, he should be surprised in his turn.

"I will not give in!" she said aloud. "I will fight him, even if it kills me, to the very last breath I draw!"

It was agony to take a bath and feel the water sting the weals on her back and the spur marks on her shoulder. The pain seemed to increase with every minute that passed.

When Lorinda dressed for dinner she deliberately chose one of the most attractive gowns that had come from London and the maid arranged her hair in a new and even more fantastic coiffure.

She wished she had some jewellery to wear because she thought it would make her appearance even more glittering and spectacular.

She draped an embroidered scarf over the bare back of her dress and carried a flirtatious little fan which had been painted by a master hand.

Slowly she walked down the stairs five minutes before dinner was due, conscious even though she looked composed that her heart was beating tumultuously.

It was more difficult than she had anticipated to encounter her husband and defy him by appearing quite normal and unconcerned.

Every instinct in her body made her long to rage at him, to tell him what she thought of him, and hope that she would humiliate him by doing so.

Then she told herself the way she had chosen was far more subtle.

By now he would have recovered from his loss of

temper and perhaps be feeling ashamed of the manner in which he had attacked her.

Surely no man who called himself a gentleman could feel otherwise?

But was he a gentleman? she asked herself scornfully. Or was his dignity and distinctive appearance merely a superficial veneer?

Underneath he might be just a plebeian, as she had suspected—a tradesman who wanted an aristocratic wife?

The scorn she felt made her carry herself more proudly, and yet despite every resolution she was nervous as the footman opened the door for her to enter the Salon.

To her surprise and indeed to her relief, she saw that her husband was not alone.

The Vicar who had married them was standing with him at the end of the room with a glass of madeira in his hand.

Lorinda advanced slowly towards them.

"I am afraid I forgot to tell you, Lorinda," Durstan said as she approached nearer, "that the Reverend Augustine Trevagan is our guest this evening."

"How delightful to see you, Vicar!" Lorinda said, holding out her hand.

"I am honoured, My Lady, in that your husband tells me I am your first guest."

"You are indeed, and as you married us, what could be more appropriate?" Lorinda asked.

She forced herself to smile sweetly at Durstan Hayle as she spoke and hoped he was embarrassed and perhaps disconcerted at her performance.

They went in to dinner and the conversation was all about some improvements that were to be made to the Church and which were to be paid for by Durstan.

The dinner was long and drawn out, and as course succeeded course Lorinda began to feel suddenly very tired.

The defiance which had made her come downstairs and face the man who had assaulted her ebbed away as her back stiffened and became more painful every minute.

The spur marks on her shoulder throbbed more than the weals from the whip and, combined, the pain was so intolerable that she was unable to eat anything.

She pushed the food about her plate and when she tried to put even the smallest amount into her mouth she felt it would choke her.

She drank a little wine, but that seemed if anything to intensify the feeling that she was sinking through the floor rather than sitting on the chair.

'I must get upstairs,' Lorinda thought to herself.

She was determined that after the effort she had made, sheer weakness should not betray her.

But she had eaten nothing since breakfast and the long walk home leading Ayshea had both physically and mentally exhausted her.

The talk had now turned to stained-glass windows.

Durstan seemed to be very knowledgeable on this subject and he and the Vicar discussed the merits of various types of glass and what would be most appropriate to the period of the Church.

It was all incredibly dull, but Lorinda knew that she would have found a conversation between the wittiest and most learned men in the country difficult to follow at this particular moment.

At last the final course was served, the decanter of port was placed in front of Durstan, and the servants withdrew.

This was the moment, Lorinda knew, when she would be expected to retire to the Salon.

She would no longer have to go on holding herself straight, pretending to be interested in what was being said while ignoring the pain which threatened to overwhelm her.

"I will ... leave you ... gentlemen to your ... port," she managed to say.

Then she thought in a sudden panic that she would be unable to rise from the table.

She managed it, but the pain in her back made her feel as if she could not focus her eyes. There was a fog rising from her feet which made everything in the Dining-Room seem very far away.

Durstan walked before her to open the door.

She could hardly see him and there was a thumping in her ears which was like the beat of drums.

'I will not . . . give in! I will . . . not!' Lorinda thought to herself. 'He is . . . waiting to see me . . . fail. He wants to . . . crow over me, and I will not . . . permit it!'

Her feet seemed like heavy weights, and yet she forced them forward one after the other. At one moment she imagined she was walking with Ayshea, then she realised it was not the horse who stood beside her but her husband.

She passed through the door. She had made it! She had won!

Then as she heard it close behind her she let the darkness cover her completely and sank almost gratefully into an unconsciousness where she no longer had to think or feel.

She was not aware that Durstan had heard the soft thud she made as she collapsed onto the carpet.

He opened the Dining-Room door again and bending down picked her up in his arms and carried her upstairs to her bed-room.

CHAPTER SIX

Lorinda awoke and lay still, remembering what had happened the night before.

She had returned to partial consciousness as she was being taken upstairs.

She knew who carried her, and, strangely enough, instead of being repelled by her husband's encircling arms she felt a sense of protection and security.

She was not thinking clearly, and yet when he set her down gently on the bed she had an impulse to hold on to him and beg him not to leave her.

Then she remembered how she had suffered at his hands, and kept her eyes closed.

He pulled the bell violently and a moment later when a maid came hurrying she heard him say:

"See to your Mistress—she is tired."

He walked away and Lorinda found herself listening to the sound of his footsteps descending the stairs.

She felt that she wanted to cry. Then she told herself this was a weakness resulting from her fainting fit and from what she had been through during the day.

While she was still remembering what had occurred, her maid came into the bed-room to pull back the curtains.

"It's been a terrible night, M'Lady," she remarked when she saw that Lorinda was awake. "You must have heard the storm! There's trees down in the Park and there's a rumour that several ships have been lost at sea."

Lorinda sat up in bed, although her back hurt her when she did so. She could see through the window that the sky was grey and that the branches of the trees were still bending before the wind.

"I was to tell you, M'Lady," the maid continued, "that the Master has gone out to inspect the damage and won't be back till lunch-time."

With a sigh of relief Lorinda lay back against the pillows.

This meant that she could rest, and she knew that despite the fact that she had slept from sheer exhaustion she still felt very tired.

After drinking just a cup of coffee she slept again and only aroused herself to get up just before luncheon.

She had in fact been downstairs only for a few minutes before Durstan returned.

He came into the Salon where she was waiting and she looked at him apprehensively. This was the first time they had been alone together since he had whipped her.

She was feeling too limp to start another quarrel, and her eyes were very large in her face as he advanced across the room towards her.

"The damage is not as bad as I feared, but bad enough," he said in a conversational tone. "There are two barns which have been blown down on one farm, and slates from the roofs have been strewn in every direction."

He walked to the grog-tray to pour himself a glass of sherry.

"May I offer you a glass of madeira?" he enquired politely.

"No, thank you," Lorinda answered.

"The sea has done the worst damage of all," he continued. "There have been dangerous cliff-falls in many

places and the smugglers will have to find a new
haven to unload their merchandise."

Lorinda was suddenly still.

"The smugglers?" she repeated.

He looked at her with a smile on his lips.

"It is impossible now for a boat to enter Keverne
Cove."

She looked at him and was suddenly still.

"It was you!" she exclaimed. "You . . . in the wood!"

"I wondered when you would realise that."

"But . . . why? Why should you have interfered?
What had it to do with . . . you?"

He walked to the hearth-rug to stand beside her.

"I guessed what you were about to do," he said after
a moment.

"It was not your business . . . when you did not
even . . . know me."

Durstan did not speak for a moment. Then he said:

"I know some of the smugglers. In fact they work on
the Estate. They are brave fellows and I would not
interfere with what is a traditional Cornish pastime,
but they are rough and at times brutal."

"They would not have harmed me," Lorinda said
proudly.

His eyes were on her face as he replied slowly:

"You could not be sure of that."

"All I wished to do was to invest my money with
them . . . no other involvement."

Durstan smiled, then he said:

"You must seldom look in your mirror."

She stared at him in astonishment, but before she
could reply, the Butler announced luncheon.

While they ate their meal, which was a light one,
Lorinda found it difficult to credit that he had actually paid her the first compliment she had ever received
from him.

They talked mostly of the storm and of the effect of
the rough sea on the cliffs.

She remembered that the granite formation of the
Cornish cliffs had a slate cover which decomposed
when exposed to the air.

It resulted in the strange and unusual appearance of the ancient rocks which were unique in Britain but they could result in land-slides which were exceedingly dangerous for those who ventured too near the edge.

"The storm is over, thank goodness!" Durstan said as he finished his meal. "But the sea is very rough and I am afraid, judging by what is being thrown up by the waves, that more than one ship was wrecked last night."

"Are they looking out for survivors?" Lorinda enquired.

"They will do so as soon as it is calm enough."

They rose from the table and Durstan walked away to where a horse was waiting for him outside the front door.

Brutus followed him, but Caesar remained with Lorinda.

He had come to her room early that morning, scratching at the door until she let him in, and had lain down beside her bed.

She bent now to pat his head and as he looked up at her she said:

"I will take you for a walk."

He looked alert at the words and she hurried upstairs to put on a short jacket over her summer gown, and a hat which had ribbons to hold it securely beneath her chin.

The wind had dropped and was less boisterous.

As Lorinda and Caesar set off through the gardens, she saw that the storm had blown the blossoms from the shrubs and there were branches of trees lying on the lawns which the gardeners were beginning to clear away.

Having exhausted the gardens, Lorinda wandered through the shrubberies and into the wood, until she heard the sound of the waves and realised that at this particular point she was not far from the sea.

Climbing a rising incline, she had her first glimpse of it.

In the sunshine it was emerald and azure blue with

white-crested waves tossing themselves impetuously
as far as the horizon.

The wind blew Lorinda's skirt round her and she
put up her hands to hold on to her hat.

At the same time, it was quite warm and there was
something buoyant and invigorating about it which
she liked.

Her mind was still busy with the discovery that it
had been Durstan who had captured her in the wood
at dawn and put a stop to her intention of negotiating
with the smugglers.

She wished she had asked him why he was there,
how he had first suspected who she was although
she'd been wearing boy's attire, and why because of
her looks he had prevented her from speaking to the
smugglers.

That was really the most pertinent question.

Could it possibly be true that in spite of the con-
tempt and indifference that she had always seen on
his face he really admired her a little?

She could not believe it.

No man who found her attractive could have behaved as her husband had done, and yet at last he had
paid her a compliment, if a somewhat strange one.

"He is so unpredictable . . . so difficult to understand," she told herself with a sigh.

She walked on until she realised that she was near
the edge of the cliffs and should go no farther.

She was well aware that Durstan had spoken the
truth when he said the cliffs were dangerous, especially after a storm.

She could remember when she was a child never
being allowed to go too near the precipitous granite
cliffs which were nearest to the Priory.

Nevertheless, the sea was an enchantment. She
stood looking at it and thinking there was no painter
who could really capture faithfully the beauty of the
waves.

A sharp bark startled her and she looked round for
Caesar.

The bark came again and with a feeling of sick hor-

ror she realised that it came from ahead and from the
very cliffs themselves.

She moved forward a few steps and realised what
had happened.

Circling round, with his nose to the ground, Caesar
had gone too close to the edge of the cliff. It had given
way beneath him and precipitated him onto a ledge
several feet down.

On her knees, Lorinda crawled over the rough
ground to where she could see him plainly.

He was safe enough where he was, but below him
was a sheer drop almost to sea level.

Inch by inch she moved forward until she could
reach her arm over the edge, but Caesar was lower
than she had thought at first and she could not touch
him.

"Sit!" she commanded.

Obediently he sat down, looking at her with trust-
ing eyes while Lorinda frantically wondered how she
could save him.

It was impossible for her to climb down to the dog
and equally impossible to catch hold of him by his
collar and drag him up to her as a man might have
done.

She thought quickly and made up her mind.

"Sit, Caesar!" she ordered again. "Good dog! On
guard!"

She knew he understood because she had heard
Durstan giving him the same orders and he had remained still, sitting without moving until the command was changed.

Praying he would do as he was told, Lorinda slowly
backed away and when she thought the ground was
safe, rose to her feet.

It was a question of time, she thought, before she
could find anybody, and Caesar might get bored with
obeying her orders when she was no longer there.

The Castle seemed a long distance away, but she
began to run back along the path they had come.

She had nearly reached the wood when she saw

below her a figure on horse-back whom she recognised.

She shouted but the wind carried her voice away and she was sure she could not be heard.

Then she pulled off her hat and waved it wildly, watching the rider on the big black horse below her, which she recognised as Akbar.

She was calling and waving but it was some seconds before she attracted his attention.

She saw Durstan's head turn, and with a feeling of utter relief watched him galloping towards her.

Before he had time to ask what was the matter she told him in a quick, breathless voice:

"Caesar! He has . . . fallen over the . . . cliff and I cannot . . . reach him. Oh, please . . . Durstan, come and . . . save him!"

"Of course!"

He bent towards her as he spoke, she raised her arms, and he swung her up onto the saddle in front of him.

He held her closely with his left arm, guiding Akbar with his right hand.

"Which way did you go?" he asked.

She pointed to the path she had followed, which was little more than a sheep-track, and Durstan followed it.

"I do not know how it happened," Lorinda said unhappily. "I was standing looking at the waves and Caesar must have been nosing round when the cliff gave way beneath him."

She was so perturbed and anxious that she was hardly conscious of the fact that she was close in her husband's arms and that because she had removed her hat, soft tendrils of her hair were blowing untidily round her pale cheeks.

"I told him to be on guard," she went on in a worried voice. "I am sure if he does not move he will be quite safe. Do you think he will obey me?"

"I am sure he will," Durstan answered gently.

They reached the top of the incline and he drew Akbar to a standstill.

"He is there . . . just over there!" Lorinda said, pointing.

Durstan swung himself from the saddle and lifted her to the ground. Then he tied Akbar to the stump of a dead tree which had not survived a previous gale.

"Stay here!" he said to Lorinda.

Then setting his hat on the ground, he moved forward, until as he neared the cliff edge he did as she had done, and went down on his knees, finally to lie full out on the wet ground.

She heard him speak to Caesar and felt a surge of relief because the dog had not moved.

As she watched, her hand on Akbar's neck, she saw Durstan move farther forward. Then slowly and very carefully he climbed over the edge of the cliff itself.

"Be careful! Be careful!" she cried impulsively.

But he paid no heed, disappearing so that all she could see was the top of his dark head.

Almost afraid to breathe, Lorinda waited and a moment later she saw Caesar appear, having been thrown up and over the top of the cliff.

"Caesar!" she called.

The dog ran to her and she put her arms round him, holding him against her, more glad than she could express in words that he was safe.

But she looked apprehensively towards the edge of the cliff, waiting for Durstan to reappear.

She saw his head and his hands grasping the edge. Then as she watched she heard him shout and there was a rumble of sound, clear and ominous above the wash of the waves.

For a moment she could not move. Then with her heart beating wildly, her lips dry, she began to crawl towards the point where he had rescued Caesar.

"On guard!" she ordered over her shoulder to the dog in a voice that seemed to be strangled in her throat.

As he obeyed her she moved as quickly as she dared to the edge of the cliff.

She looked down and gave a gasp.

It was all too easy to see what had happened.

The ledge on which Caesar had sat and where Durstan must have stood to rescue him. had given way.

Far below at the bottom of the cliffs, almost on the edge of the waves, she could see his body sprawled on the rocks.

He had fallen on his back and the avalanche of stones he had started half-covered his body.

Time itself stood still as Lorinda looked down in horror. Then she knew—she must save him!

She crawled back from the edge of the cliff and ran to Akbar.

She released his bridle from the stump of the tree and mounted him without difficulty, thankful that her wide skirt enabled her to ride astride.

Followed by Caesar, she rode as fast as she could back along the path through the wood towards the Castle.

It did not take very long, but it seemed to Lorinda as if hours had passed before she reached the stables to tell the groom what had occurred and send someone in search of the Agent.

He came hurrying from the Castle.

"Is it true, M'Lady, that Mr. Hayle has fallen over the cliffs?" he enquired.

"He was saving Caesar," Lorinda said briefly. "He is lying unconscious at the foot of them. Is it possible to get to him by boat?"

"It will be quite impossible until the sea is smoother," the Agent replied. "A boat would be dashed against the rocks in a matter of seconds."

"Then we must try with ropes," Lorinda said. "I have already ordered the grooms to find them."

She saw by the Agent's face that he thought that this might prove to be even more difficult, but she merely said sharply:

"I require blankets, a pillow, a flask of brandy—and quickly!"

"Yes, of course, M'Lady."

The Agent hurried to obey her commands, and the grooms were saddling horses and bringing them from the stables. Caesar was taken into the Castle.

Finally Lorinda led the way back, still riding Akbar. Six men accompanied her on horseback, one of them carrying the blankets she had ordered.

She stopped where they had stopped before, but this time two of the grooms remained with the horses while Lorinda showed the Agent and the others how to approach the cliff.

They looked over and saw that Durstan was lying where she had last seen him.

The waves were breaking tempestuously against the rocks and Lorinda knew that the Agent had spoken the truth when he had said that it would be impossible for a boat to reach him.

"Bring the ropes a little to the left," she said. "The cliff looks firmer there."

"I doubt it, M'Lady," the Agent replied. "After a storm such as we had last night, the slate crumbles at the touch, and as you already know, it is dangerous to go near to the edge."

"I will explain what I want you to do," Lorinda replied.

She walked ahead of the men and they followed her, ready, she felt, to argue about everything she suggested.

Then coming to a standstill she said firmly:

"I want you to tie the ropes round me and hold on to them from here. I shall start climbing down the cliff. Until you hear me shout, you must keep a steady strain on me."

"It is impossible, M'Lady!" the Agent expostulated. "I cannot allow you to do this. One of us will go."

"I am much the lightest," Lorinda replied, "and I intend to reach Mr. Hayle. You will please do exactly as I have said."

She turned towards the grooms as she spoke and ordered them to fasten a loop of rope round her waist.

"When I reach the bottom," she said, "I will want you to throw down the blankets as near as possible to

where the Master is lying. Do not come near the edge
of the cliff or you may cause a fall of stones. I will
take the flask with me."

She put it in the pocket of her jacket, then began to
move towards the edge.

"I cannot allow you to do this, M'Lady!" the Agent
cried. "It is madness! You may injure yourself—perhaps seriously!"

"I climbed these cliffs when I was a child," Lorinda
answered, "and I am not afraid. Just do as I have told
you."

She crawled to the edge, then very cautiously, holding on to the ropes, she let herself over.

At first it was difficult to find a foothold. Then she
began to descend, knowing that the ropes would keep
her from falling. At the same time, she was anxious not
to dislodge another avalanche.

Slowly she went down, sometimes slipping on the
wet, decomposing slate, sometimes feeling as if she
was suspended in mid-air, her fingers slipping on everything she touched.

Finally she reached the firmness of the rocks below and freed herself from the ropes.

She gave a shout and looking up saw the Agent
watching her from a little way along the cliff.

He had been wise enough not to stand directly
above her. She waved and he waved in response.

Then she started to pick her way carefully over the
slippery rocks, which were wet from the waves, to
where Durstan was lying.

It was not as easy as she had thought, for there were
deep crevices. There was also an anxious moment
when she thought she was slipping into the sea.

The spray in her face sometimes blinded her and
she had to wipe her eyes before she could proceed,
but finally she reached him.

He was lying very still and she wondered in a sudden terror if perhaps he was dead.

There was a wound which was bleeding on his forehead, caused no doubt by a large stone. As she began
to brush away the stones which half-covered him she

wondered how many bones had been broken by his fall.

She thought perhaps his riding-boots would have saved him from breaking an ankle, if nothing else.

He was not wet, but getting damper all the time from the spray of the waves.

She looked up when she heard a shout and found that the bundle of blankets had fallen only about six feet away.

She took the cord from them, covered him with two blankets, and very gently inserted the pillow under his head.

He was completely unconscious, but she wondered if she should try to pour a little brandy between his lips. Then she decided against it.

She had moved all the stones from his body and now felt beneath him to see if he was lying on any large ones which might make him more uncomfortable.

There was really nothing more she could do.

She realised the sun had gone in and it was late in the afternoon. This meant, she knew, that they would have to spend the night here.

It would be impossible even if the sea dropped in an hour or two for anyone to get a boat in to the foot of the cliffs.

There were many half-submerged rocks which it would be impossible to avoid unless it was daylight.

Lorinda was quite certain that the Agent would do everything possible to effect a rescue the following day.

For the moment, she had not only to keep Durstan alive but also prevent herself from suffering from exposure.

She touched first his hands, then his face, very gently.

With his eyes shut he looked younger, she thought, and very much less frightening than he had seemed to her at other times.

In fact she felt there was something almost pathetic about him now that he was no longer authoritative and imperious, frightening her with his air of command.

Instead he was just a man who was suffering, through her fault.

It was almost hurtful to think of it, and yet it was true. She was to blame for walking to the cliffs with Caesar.

If she had had any sense she would have realised the danger and put the dog on a lead.

"Everything I have done since I married has been wrong," Lorinda told herself with a little sob.

She remembered her behaviour of yesterday, and the cruelty she had inflicted upon Ayshea.

She shivered now not from the cold but from the accusations she brought against herself. How could she have been so unrestrained, so unpleasant?

"I will never," she vowed, "ever wear . . . a spur again . . . never!"

Instinctively because she was so unhappy she moved a little closer to Durstan.

She wondered how badly he was hurt and remembered in horror that eight years ago two boys from the village had fallen from the cliffs when bird-nesting, and been killed.

"They were young," she told herself, "Durstan is a man."

Yet she was afraid.

It grew darker and now she told herself the only sensible thing to do was to keep as close as she could to her husband so that at least their bodies would keep each other warm.

The easiest way was to slip her arm at the back of his neck and bring him closer to her so that they could share the pillow.

She had covered him with two blankets and now she covered them both with the third, pulling it over her head and leaving just their faces exposed to the air so that they could breathe.

Her arms went round him, holding him close, and as darkness fell she could no longer see him but only feel the heaviness of his head against her breast.

"It will be . . . all right," she whispered as if she were speaking to a child. "If you have broken any bones they will . . . heal, and although the fall gave you . . . concussion, that will go . . . away in a few days."

She could hear her own voice murmuring above the noise of the waves and because it was somehow comforting in the darkness she went on talking.

"You are so strong . . . stronger than most men . . . so this will not do you any permanent damage . . . although you may be in . . . pain for a little . . . while."

It was very dark, there were no stars, but suddenly Lorinda felt afraid, not of the night, but that Durstan might have died while she was holding him.

He was so still and she put her hand against his cold cheek, then slipping it beneath his coat she undid the buttons of his shirt, feeling frantically for his heart.

It was beating and she gave a sob of thankfulness.

It did not seem strange or wrong to be touching the naked body of a man and she left her hand there, feeling the warmth and the smoothness of his skin.

"It is . . . all right," she whispered. "You are . . . alive. You will . . . live!"

She moved her face towards his as she spoke and felt his cheek cool against the softness of hers.

"You must . . . live!" she said. "You . . . must! I want you to!"

She was suddenly still, surprised by her own words.

Then she knew that what she had just said was the truth. She wanted him to live! She wanted to be with him and she no longer hated him!

Her arm beneath his head was cramped but she would not move.

As the long hours of darkness passed Lorinda did not sleep. Instead she felt that only by staying awake could she protect and watch over the man she held.

It gave her a strange feeling, one she had never known before, to hold him close. For the first time in her life she was not revolted by the proximity of a man.

'He needs me,' she thought to herself, 'and no-one

in the world can give him what I am giving him at this moment.'

'She felt as if her whole being went out to succour him, to keep him alive, and that only by giving him some indivisible part of herself could this be accomplished.

Once she almost dropped off to sleep, then roused herself to feel frantically once again for his heart.

She felt that somehow she had betrayed him by not continuing to give him the strength which she felt flowed from her body into his.

Before the dawn came she found herself praying.

"Make him well, God! Let there be no . . . ill effects from his fall . . . from the cold, or from the fact that he is damp from the sea. Take care of him, protect him as I have tried to do."

It was a prayer that came from the very depths of her heart.

Vaguely, as if someone was trying to comfort her, she remembered hearing that the dampness of sea water was not as dangerous as that of rain.

Besides, she had kept him warm—she was sure of it!

The sky was lightening and she knew that during the night, when she had only been able to hear the waves and not been able to see them, the sound of their breaking against the cliffs had grown quieter until it died away into a mere murmur.

Now a pale translucent light began to sweep away the darkness and Lorinda realised there was very little motion on the sea.

Gone were the white-crested waves, gone the great showers of spray as they broke over the rocks.

Instead there was just a soft lap of the incoming tide and she knew that it would not be long before they would be rescued.

Her hand was still against Durstan's heart and she thought that though he would never know how this night had been spent, she would never be able to forget it.

"I have looked after you," she said softly.

She thought as she spoke that he might be her son rather than her husband.

He had needed her and she had not failed him, and he had been lying in her arms as helpless as any baby.

She wondered what it would be like to hold her own child.

'When I have one,' she thought, 'I will never let it feel unwanted.'

Unwanted she herself had always been. It still hurt to remember how her father had resented her being a girl instead of a boy and had shown her no affection but often a positive dislike.

Nor had her mother wanted her love. Completely engrossed in her husband, she always made it obvious that Lorinda should have been the son they'd never had.

"I have never had anyone to love," Lorinda told herself.

That, she thought with a sudden perception, was what had made her determined to assert herself, to show the world she did not care.

"I am self-sufficient! I have myself and that is all I want!"

Frequently she had shouted it aloud.

But it had been untrue! She had longed to give her love to someone who needed it.

Not passion—that was a different thing and frightened her—but a deep selfless love which was more spiritual than physical.

A love that a woman could give to her child or to a man who needed not only her body but her very soul.

"That is what I have always wanted," she told herself.

She felt the first fingers of the sun glimmer in her eyes and she raised her head.

Rounding the point she saw a boat with six oarsmen coming towards them.

Now they could go home!

As the oarsmen brought in the boat until it was almost directly below them, Lorinda gently raised herself and began to move her numbed arm from beneath Durstan's head.

As she did so, she realised that she wanted to stay where she was because she loved him!

* * *

The next few days, Lorinda remembered later, were a nightmare of anxiety.

The Doctor was fetched from Falmouth, who was, the Agent assured her, the most experienced man available within the vicinity of a hundred miles.

But he seemed to Lorinda to know very little about the effects that such a fall could have on a man of Durstan's size and age.

"He may have two or three ribs broken—I cannot be sure," he said. "He is certainly a mass of bruises and his left wrist is badly sprained."

"He has not regained consciousness," Lorinda said after the third day.

The Doctor shrugged his shoulders.

"Concussion is a strange thing, My Lady, and your husband is a big man. If he fell on his head there might be complications."

"What sort of complications?" Lorinda insisted.

The Doctor was very vague.

He talked of cerebral hemorrhage, said it was difficult to diagnose, and told a long story about a patient who had been unconscious for three weeks after an accident, and had then suffered from temporary blindness.

This was hardly encouraging, but Lorinda finally came to the conclusion that he knew very little about anything that was not an open wound.

When he left she went up to Durstan's bed-room to look despairingly at him lying still and silent, his mind beyond her reach.

Durstan's valet, a small wiry little man called Gribbon, who had been with him for years, was a tower of strength and encouragement.

"The Master'll be all right, M'Lady," he said when he saw Lorinda looking so despondent. "I've nursed him through malaria, typhoid fever, and a lot of other nasty Indian fevers, and when they were over he bobbed up again like a floating cork!"

"He looks so pale," Lorinda murmured, "and naturally he has grown thinner."

"He was skin and bone after one bout he had in India," Gribbon said cheerfully, "but he soon ate it all back, so to speak! Don't you worry, M'Lady, we'll get 'im on his feet again."

Lorinda knew that even if they had wished to engage one, it was impossible in that part of the world to find Nurses, and indeed in any part of England.

They were usually drunken old midwives whom no decent person would employ in the house.

She felt it was therefore up to her to nurse her husband. But Gribbon had very strong ideas on the matter and finally she conceded a great deal of what he thought of, she realised, as "his rights."

Gribbon washed Durstan and looked after him in the morning while Lorinda slept, having been with him at night.

She would come back "on duty," as Gribbon called it, at tea-time after she had walked in the garden with Caesar and Brutus. It was important for her to have fresh air even if their patient could get none.

"We can't have you knocking yourself up, M'Lady," Gribbon would say with the affectionate sternness of a Nanny coping with a rather difficult child.

It was Gribbon who had the idea that even while Durstan was unconscious music might reach him.

"Why don't you play to him, M'Lady?"

"Do you mean play the piano?"

"The Master's fond of music. Always has been."

"I had no idea," Lorinda murmured.

"There was a lady in India he used to like listening to. Very skilful she was. You never knows—although he seems far away from us, perhaps a tune will reach him while our voices can't."

Lorinda gave the order for a piano to be set up in the Boudoir which lay between the King's and the Queen's Rooms.

She realised from the way the room was furnished

that it must have been intended as a woman's room, for there was nothing masculine in the soft colours of the curtains and the beautiful furniture which echoed and complemented that in her own bed-room.

The piano was put in one corner, and she left the door open into her husband's room so that she could see him as she played.

She was unlikely, she thought to herself, to equal the lady he had listened to in India, and she felt an unmistakable pang of jealousy as she wondered who the lady could have been.

It did not sound as if she was one of the dark-eyed houris who had relieved his loneliness.

"How little I know of him," she said, and sighed, and added that what she did know was principally that he disapproved of her and everything she did.

Yet, at the same time, he had wanted to marry her, and because she now loved him she began to pray that it was not entirely because he had wanted the Priory Estate or an aristocratic wife.

Seeing him lying straight and still in the bed, she told herself it was unthinkable that he could be anything but as well born as she was herself. There was nothing in the least plebeian or commonplace about him.

A week after the accident, Lorinda came back to the Castle from her walk with the dogs.

"It is a lovely day," she said to the Butler as she entered the Hall.

"There is a gentleman from London asking to see the Master, M'Lady. I told him he was ill and he said he would be grateful if he could speak to you."

"A gentleman from London?" Lorinda asked in surprise.

"I think he has business with the Master, M'Lady."

"He would not wish to see Mr. Ashwin?" Lorinda suggested, thinking that the Agent or perhaps Durstan's secretary could deal with this better than she could.

"No, M'Lady, he was most insistent that he must see either the Master or yourself."

"Very well, I will see him."

She was impatient because she wanted so much to go upstairs to find out how her patient was since she had left him.

The Butler showed her into the Library and she found there an elderly, grey-haired man who rose as she appeared.

"Good-afternoon," Lorinda said politely.

"You are Lady Lorinda Hayle, I believe?"

"I am!"

"I have come from Hickman, Links, and Hickman," the man explained. "I am in fact Mr. Ebenezer Hickman. We are Attorneys to Lord Penryn."

Lorinda looked surprised.

"Lord Penryn?" she questioned.

Mr. Hickman smiled.

"I believe he still calls himself Durstan Hayle, as he did when he left England; but he is in fact Lord Penryn, and has been for the last six years!"

Lorinda drew in her breath.

"Are you saying that my husband is Lord Penryn?" she asked. "Of the same family who owned this Castle?"

"He inherited the title on his father's death, My Lady, but he was in India at the time. I understand he had preferred not to use his title since he returned."

"Why?" Lorinda asked.

Mr. Hickman smiled.

"I am sure His Lordship would rather tell you the story himself, but there was some altercation with his father as to whether he should leave England and seek his fortune elsewhere."

He paused.

"Very incensed the old gentleman was at the time, and I believe he accused his son of being willing to exploit the family name commercially."

Mr. Hickman smiled again.

"Knowing your husband, My Lady, you will be well aware that nothing would annoy him more. He took

the name of Durstan Hayle and made his fortune
without the assistance of the family name."

Lorinda found it difficult to speak.

She could only remember the times she had jeered
at Durstan because she had thought he had married
her because he wanted an aristocratic wife.

The Cambornes were an old Cornish family, but not
nearly as old or as distinguished, despite their superior title, as the Penryns.

The Penryns were part of the history of Cornwall
and their glorious deeds had reverberated down the
centuries.

With difficulty Lorinda managed to say:

"Why did you wish to see me, Mr. Hickman?"

He drew some papers which looked like Deeds
from the black bag he carried.

"I have here the papers made out according to His
Lordship's instructions," he said, "and both His Lordship's signature and yours are required on them."

"What are they?" Lorinda asked.

Mr. Hickman looked surprised.

"They consist, My Lady, of the Deed of Gift of one
hundred thousand pounds, which His Lordship has
made over to you unconditionally, and also the Deeds
concerning the house in London which is allotted to
your use for your life-time."

Lorinda felt as though the Attorney's words were
blows that struck at her very heart.

Durstan was making her independent! Durstan in
fact was making arrangements so that he could be rid
of her!

She felt as if the room swung round her and she put
her hand on the desk to steady herself.

"I do not . . . want the . . . money or the . . . house."

The lawyer looked down at his papers.

"I expect you feel like that, My Lady, because you
have not been married for long. You feel that nothing
could ever come between you, that as in a fairy-story
you will live happily ever after."

He paused, then said:

"But after a long life of experience I have always thought, My Lady, it is wise for a woman to be independent. Whatever happens in the future, whatever difficulties you may encounter, you will be your own mistress, and you will have a roof over your head."

He was not being impertinent, Lorinda knew, he was speaking in the kindly way that an elderly man might speak to an impetuous girl who had no idea of the difficulties and troubles which marriage could bring her.

She thought perhaps Mr. Hickman was also aware that her husband could be not only a difficult man but an unpredictable one.

He had certainly continued to surprise her, she thought, ever since she had met him, and now this was perhaps the greatest surprise of all.

He was in fact prepared to set her free, to let her go after he had gone to such pains to make her his wife.

She thought how gladly she would have welcomed such a generous gift a week ago.

Then she would have taken the money, accepted the house, and gone back to London to leave behind the hatred she had felt in the Castle.

But now everything was different!

She could not leave. In fact she would not leave!

She made up her mind.

"Thank you, Mr. Hickman, for coming here," she said. "I am sorry you should have had this long journey to no avail, but my husband has had a very serious accident. Until he recovers and until we can talk this over together, nothing can be done."

"I heard from the Butler that His Lordship was too ill to see me," Mr. Hickman said, "and of course in the circumstances there is nothing I can do but wait until His Lordship is well enough."

"Thank you again for coming," Lorinda said. "I hope we may offer you a meal before you leave, and if you wish to stay the night there is of course plenty of accommodation in the Castle."

As he expressed his thanks she moved quickly away and hurried up the stairs to the King's Room.

She had a frantic feeling that perhaps already the door was barred against her and she would not be able to see Durstan again.

But as she entered the room, Gribbon, who was sitting by the bed-side, sprang to his feet.

"He's come round, M'Lady!"

"When?"

"Half an hour ago."

"He was really conscious?"

"Yes, M'Lady, but a little bewildered-like, though speaking quite sensible."

"What did he say?" Lorinda asked.

"He just says: 'What the hell has happened to me, Gribbon?' I gave him something to drink and he went back to sleep again."

"That means that his brain is not damaged," Lorinda said almost beneath her breath.

She went down on her knees beside the bed. Her heart was singing with gratitude.

"Thank You, God ... thank You!" she found herself whispering.

CHAPTER SEVEN

Lorinda struck a soft chord, then rose from the piano to walk into the King's Room.

Durstan was sitting in an armchair and when she reached his side she saw that he was asleep.

He had already been out for a drive that morning, and although she had suggested he should rest he had refused her scornfully.

The Doctor had announced earlier in the week that there was no need for further visiting by him.

"Your husband's as good as new, My Lady," he declared, laughing at his own joke, but he had also insisted that Durstan must take things easily for another week or so.

"Plenty of fresh air, but not too much riding," had been his last instructions as he drove away in an ancient gig that was known all over the county.

But it had not been easy to persuade Durstan to obey him.

While he had been ill and in bed Lorinda had been able to impose her will on him, but now he was back in the saddle and he would do what he wished to do.

Looking down at him asleep, she thought that she loved him more with every passing day.

137

She knew it was because he had needed her and she could give him the love and care that no-one had ever asked of her before.

Although he had regained consciousness a week after the accident and she had been able to coax him into taking a little food, he had in fact been desperately ill.

At times Lorinda had even felt that he might slip away from her in his sleep and she would find that his heart had ceased to beat.

It was then that she felt as she had when she'd held him close to her on the rocks, that she could give him some of her own strength, and that the life-force she poured out kept him living.

But gradually he began to grow stronger.

If he had broken some ribs, as the Doctor suspected, they must have knit, and the bruises faded from his body, including the terrible wound on his forehead.

He did not wish to talk very much and she thought that his head often ached unbearably, although he would never say so.

He liked to hear her play and he would listen until the music soothed him into a deep sleep as it had done now.

Lorinda had deliberately kept from him anything which might worry or upset him.

Through Mr. Ashwin, the Agent, she was in touch with all that was happening on the Estate, and she made decisions and gave orders of which she thought her husband would approve.

But she was determined not to discuss anything controversial with him until he was really well.

Instead, she took him news of the horses and brought him great bunches of flowers from the garden. Sometimes he liked her to read to him.

Once he had said to her:

"Who taught you to play so well?"

"You flatter me!" she said with a smile. "I know how much I lack musically. I engaged a teacher for myself when I was twelve, but there were times when my father said he was too expensive. Then I had to wait until a winning streak enabled me to employ him again."

"So you chose your own education," Durstan said slowly.

"I wish I had known how important learning could be," she said, and sighed.

She went on to tell him how when he was ill and spent most of the day and night sleeping she had gone to the great Library to find a book to read.

"I was appalled at the number of them and the realisation of how much there was I did not know," she said with a smile.

"What was your final choice?" he asked.

"I found out how little the one Governess I had, who was very underpaid, had taught me about the world."

"So where did you start to find out about it?" Durstan questioned.

"I started with India because you . . ."

Lorinda stopped. She felt that what she had been about to say would be too revealing, and added hastily:

"Gribbon has talked so much about that country that I was naturally interested."

She did not tell him that the book she had found in the Library had exquisite paintings of Rajput dancing-girls.

When she had looked at them she felt an agonising jealousy because she thought that theirs was the type of beauty that Durstan most admired.

But whether he admired her or not, she had known that she was necessary to him, and as she nursed him, waited on him, and anticipated his every wish, she knew that she had never been so happy.

This was what she had always wanted of life, to be wanted and to be able to give someone she cared for not her beauty but her inner self.

Now she moved very softly away from Durstan's chair to sit nearby.

She sat looking at him as if she felt that the sands

were running out and the time might come when she
would no longer be able to watch him.

Always at the back of her mind was the fear that
Mr. Hickman had engendered in her when he had
brought her the papers to sign which would make her
independent.

She had not yet mentioned his visit to Durstan, but
she knew the day would come, and it was not very
far away, when he would have to know.

"I love him!" Lorinda said to herself. "Oh, God,
make him love me a little or at least need me as he
has needed me this last month."

* * *

Dinner was finishing and the Chef had excelled
himself because it was the first time that Durstan had
dined downstairs since his accident.

No man could look more distinguished than he did
in his evening-clothes, and he also appeared, Lorinda
thought, almost as well as he had before the fall.

He was a little thinner and there was still a scar on
his forehead.

Otherwise, with his meticulously tied cravat, the
blue satin of his evening-coat, and a diamond flash-
ing in his shirt, he looked exceedingly elegant and
more attractive than any other man she had ever seen.

She too had made an effort, and was wearing a
gown she thought would please him. It was in fact
not unlike the one she had worn at her wedding.

It was white and the drapery of the skirt was
caught with camelias. There were camelias also in
Lorinda's hair, which her maid had arranged in a
quiet but very becoming coiffure that had nothing
flamboyant about it.

When she moved from the table to go into the Salon, Durstan followed her.

The Butler set down a decanter of port and one of
brandy on a side-table, then withdrew.

Durstan however did not look at them. He stood
looking at her for a moment before he said:

"There is so much for which I have to thank you!"

Lorinda looked surprised.

"Thank me?" she questioned.

"I have been told that after I had fallen you climbed down the cliff to stay with me all night."

Lorinda did not speak and he asked:

"Why did you do that?"

"It was . . . my fault . . . I should not have taken Caesar . . . near the . . . edge."

"You saved my life, Lorinda! Did you want me to live?"

"Y-yes."

"Why?"

Lorinda could not meet his eyes nor find words to answer him, and after a moment he picked up a box from the side of his chair.

"I have here a present to thank you for your care of me while I was ill," he said in a different tone.

"I have no wish . . ." she began, then her voice died away because Durstan had opened the jewel-box.

There, lying on its velvet bed, was the emerald necklace which had belonged to her mother and which was the one thing which had really grieved her to lose when the house and its contents had been sold in London.

"*You* . . . bought . . . it!" she cried a little incoherently.

"For you."

He picked up the necklace as he spoke and held it out towards her.

She let him put it round her neck and she turned so that he could fasten the clasp.

"How could you have . . . bought it for . . . me?" she asked. "You had not . . . met me . . . then."

"I had seen you at a dance at Hampstead when you appeared as Lady Godiva."

"You were . . . there?"

The exclamation was low and the colour rose in her cheeks.

"I was there!" he said in a voice that she felt had something grim about it.

"You . . . were . . . shocked?"

"Appalled is a better word!"

"Then why . . . did you . . . marry me? I cannot . . . understand."

"I had just come back to England and was not expecting social behaviour to have changed so drastically. I had a wager with Lord Charlton, a friend of mine."

There was silence for a moment and Lorinda said in a voice he could hardly hear:

"W-what was . . . your bet?"

"That I would tame a tigress. He said it was impossible."

Lorinda drew in her breath.

Now she was beginning to understand what had happened, and it was an agony beyond anything she had ever suffered in her whole life.

She looked away from Durstan, trying to steady her voice and speak as if she did not feel as though she was on the rack and the pain was increasing second by second.

"So . . . it was . . . just an . . . experiment!"

"As you say—an experiment!" he agreed.

Because she felt as if the pattern was beginning to fall into place, she said in a voice that sounded strange even to herself:

"A . . . man called . . . Hickman came here . . . when you were ill."

"I imagined he would have done so."

"He told me that you are in reality . . . Lord Penryn."

"I expect he also told you why I changed my name when I went abroad."

"You do not intend to . . . revert to your real title and take your . . . place in the House of Lords?"

There was silence for a moment, then Durstan said:

"I thought perhaps I might do so, if I had a son."

Lorinda felt as if the room swung round her.

It was not the answer she had expected. Then she said:

"Mr. Hickman told me that you . . . wished to settle some . . . money on me and . . . offer me a house in . . . London."

"The Deeds are here waiting for us both to sign them."

"Why are you . . . doing this? Can it be that you are . . . intending to send me . . . away?"

It was almost impossible to say the words and because she felt the tears welling into her eyes Lorinda moved towards the side-table where there was a huge vase of flowers.

She put out her hand to touch the blossoms, knowing she dare not look at Durstan and that every nerve in her body was tense, waiting for his reply.

There was a silence that was frightening. After a moment, because she could not bear the suspense, Lorinda said:

"I had a . . . letter from Papa . . . yesterday. He is very . . . happy in . . . Ireland. I think he will never . . . wish to return to this . . . country."

"But you have many friends in London."

She thought of those who she had believed were her friends and how disloyal they had been when she was in trouble, and knew that she never wished to see any of them again.

She knew too that she could never go back. Having lived at the Castle, having been with Durstan, she could never tolerate the life she had once thought amusing.

She had the feeling that he was going to say that he no longer needed her.

She felt as if every nerve in her whole body was taut as she waited for the blow to fall and for him to speak the words by which he would destroy her last hope of happiness.

"Are you . . . sending me . . . away?"

She forced herself to ask the question, knowing she could stand the suspense no longer, feeling as if she must scream if he did not tell her what he intended.

"Come here, Lorinda!"

There was the authoritative note in his voice that she knew so well and some remnant of pride made her fight against the tears that filled her eyes.

He must never know what she was feeling. She would not embarrass him by asking for his pity!

"I told you to come here!"

His voice was deep and because she had grown used to responding to his wishes she turned obediently.

It was difficult to see him because the tears blinded her, but she would not let them fall as she moved towards him, holding her chin high.

She stopped close to him.

"I am offering you your freedom," Durstan said quietly.

She looked up at him wildly. Then the tension snapped and the last defence fell.

"I have no . . . wish to be . . . free! I want to stay with you! Please . . . do not send me . . . away. . . ."

Her voice was choked with tears and the words were almost incoherent. Then, losing the last vestige of her pride and self-control, she sobbed:

"I . . . I will . . . obey you . . . I will do . . . anything you want . . . only let me . . . st-stay. Please . . . let me . . . stay."

She hardly knew what she was doing and she would have gone down on her knees if he had not put his arms round her and drawn her close to him.

She hid her face against his shoulder and cried helplessly as a child might do.

"Why should you want to stay with me?" Durstan asked, his voice very low and deep.

"B-because . . . I love you! I love you . . . agonisingly!"

The words were spoken, and some detached part of her brain told Lorinda that this was the moment when Durstan could punish her for her hatred and defiance and for the way she had fought him ever since they had known each other.

He could laugh at her, and she knew that if he did so there would be nothing left for her but die!

She felt him tighten one arm about her, then he put his fingers under her chin and turned her face up to his.

Her mouth was blurred and trembling and she

could not see him through her tears, which were running down her cheeks, but she knew he looked at her for a long second before he said:

"There is one experiment I have not yet made and that is to kiss the woman I love!"

His lips were on hers before she could understand what he had said.

Then as his mouth took possession of her she felt something wild and wonderful sweep away her unhappiness and her tears.

It was so exquisite, so perfect, it expressed in one action all the love that she had felt these past weeks.

She felt as if his lips took from her not only the life and strength she had tried to give him, but also invaded some secret part of herself that she had not even known she possessed.

She felt him draw even closer and his lips became more possessive, more demanding, and her whole being leapt in response.

This was not only love . . . this was life, this was a divine force from God, to whom she had prayed in her extremity.

She felt the wonder and the rapture of it seep through her wave after wave and sweep away her defiance and her sense of being unwanted.

She felt as if the air was filled with celestial music and everything that was beautiful flowed between them so that they became one person.

Durstan raised his head to look down at her shining eyes and trembling lips.

"I love . . . you!" she whispered. "Oh, Durstan . . . I love . . . you!"

"Do you really think I would let you go?" he asked hoarsely.

Then he was kissing her again fiercely, passionately, demandingly, and the world disappeared.

There was only love uniting their hearts so that they were indivisible.

* * *

Lorinda rose to move silently across the darkened room to the window.

She slipped behind the closed curtains and stood at the open casement, looking out.

High overhead, the stars were fading in the sky and she knew that in a few moments the dawn would break.

She drew in a deep breath of happiness and in that moment knew she was no longer alone.

She felt Durstan's arms go round her and she put her head against his shoulder.

"I thought you were . . . asleep."

"How could you leave me and I not be aware of it?"

She moved a little closer to him as she said:

"I wanted to see the dawn breaking. It is the . . . beginning of a . . . new life."

"For us both," he said gently.

"You do . . . love me?"

"More than I can begin to tell you."

"And . . . you do . . . admire me a . . . little?"

"I have never seen anything more beautiful than your face, or more perfect than your body."

Lorinda drew in her breath. His words made her thrill.

"But there is so much more than your beauty," he went on. "There is something which reaches out from you which makes me complete in myself. Something which no-one else has ever given me."

Lorinda turned her lips against his shoulder. She understood what he was saying. It was what she had tried to give him when she had been afraid he might die.

The thought that she might have lost him made her ask:

"You will go on . . . loving me?"

"We have only just begun to love each other in this life, but we have been together in so many other lives in the past."

"Do you really believe that?"

"I have lived too long in the East not to believe in Fate, Kismet, and the Wheel of Rebirth."

She raised her face to his although it was too dark

to see anything but the vague outline of his profile against the sky.

"Did you know . . . that when you . . . first saw . . . me?"

"I knew that you belonged to me—that you were the woman I had been waiting to find for many years."

"Even though I . . . shocked you?"

"That was why you shocked me—I could not bear other men to look at your body when it was mine, as every perfect part of you was mine."

She quivered at the passion in his voice, and hid her face against his neck as she whispered:

"I was not . . . really naked. I was . . . cheating by making people . . . think so."

"And when you posed in front of Paris to gain the golden apple?"

"That was a lie. They wanted to think it was me . . . but actually I was not . . . there."

She felt Durstan give a sigh, as if the knowledge had worried him and now he was relieved of it.

"Why did you make that . . . bet?" she asked.

"Because I knew instinctively that underneath the outrageous behaviour, the flamboyance, and the disregard for all conventions, you were you, the woman I already worshipped in my heart."

"How could you have . . . known that?" she asked.

"Oh, darling, I am so ashamed that I was so blind that when I saw you I did not feel the same."

His arms tightened round her and he held her very close.

"There is plenty of time for you to show me how sorry you are," he replied. "A whole life-time, in fact!"

"I shall love you more every day," Lorinda promised. "All I want . . . is to give you . . . my love . . . and myself."

There was a note of passion in her voice that was unmistakable and Durstan kissed her hair as he said:

"As a matter of fact, I did not win my bet. I am prepared to admit that I lost it."

"You lost it?" she exclaimed.

"I found that after all one cannot tame a tigress who has red hair and green eyes which glisten in the dark."

He felt her body quiver against his. Then she whispered:

"Are you shocked that I should . . . love you so . . . overwhelmingly and that when you touch me it should . . . excite me . . . so wildly?"

He kissed her forehead.

"It is wonderful, perfect, supreme, and how I will always make you feel, my precious love," he said. "But I warn you . . ."

His fingers clasped the soft column of her neck before he went on:

"If I ever find any man looking at you except with respect I will kill him—and I will strangle you! I am jealous to the point of madness!"

Lorinda laughed from sheer happiness.

"I am not afraid! If another man exists in the whole world, then I have never seen him. There is only you . . . and you . . . and you . . ."

She lifted her lips to his and the last words were spoken against his mouth.

He crushed her to him, kissing her with a desire that could not be repressed, a passion that was like a fire leaping into flame as she responded to it.

The dawn was breaking golden over the horizon, thrusting away the darkness of the night and enveloping them both in a translucent light.

Lorinda put her arm round Durstan's neck and drew him closer still. Then as she realised she could see his eyes looking down into hers she said with a little break in her voice:

"Our new day has come . . . my darling . . . magnificent . . . husband!"

"A new day," he echoed.

Then against her lips he murmured:

"Look at me—think of me—I want you!"

He pulled her back into the room, and as the curtains fell to shut out the dawn, he picked her up in his arms.

"You are mine, my lovely one!" he said in the darkness. "Completely and absolutely mine, now and for all eternity!"

Holding her lips and her body fiercely captive, he carried her back to the bed.

ABOUT THE AUTHOR

BARBARA CARTLAND, the celebrated romantic author, historian, playwright, lecturer, political speaker and television personality, has now written over 150 books. Miss Cartland has had a number of historical books published and several biographical ones, including that of her brother, Major Ronald Cartland, who was the first Member of Parliament to be killed in the War. This book had a Foreword by Sir Winston Churchill.

In private life, Barbara Cartland, who is a Dame of the Order of St. John of Jerusalem, has fought for better conditions and salaries for Midwives and nurses. As President of the Royal College of Midwives (Hertfordshire Branch), she has been invested with the first Badge of Office ever given in Great Britain, which was subscribed to by the Midwives themselves. She has also championed the cause for old people and founded the first Romany Gypsy Camp in the world.

Barbara Cartland is deeply interested in Vitamin Therapy and is President of the British National Association for Health.

Barbara Cartland

The world's bestselling author of romantic fiction.
Her stories are always captivating tales of intrigue,
adventure and love.

☐	THE CRUEL COUNT	2128	$1.25
☐	CALL OF THE HEART	2140	$1.25
☐	AS EAGLES FLY	2147	$1.25
☐	THE MASK OF LOVE	2366	$1.25
☐	AN ARROW OF LOVE	2426	$1.25
☐	A GAMBLE WITH HEARTS	2430	$1.25
☐	A KISS FOR THE KING	2433	$1.25
☐	A FRAME OF DREAMS	2434	$1.25
☐	THE FRAGRANT FLOWER	2435	$1.25
☐	MOON OVER EDEN	2437	$1.25
☐	THE GOLDEN ILLUSION	2449	$1.25
☐	FIRE ON THE SNOW	2450	$1.25
☐	THE HUSBAND HUNTERS	2461	$1.25
☐	THE SHADOW OF SIN	6430	$1.25
☐	SAY YES, SAMANTHA	7834	$1.25
☐	THE KARMA OF LOVE	8106	$1.25
☐	BEWITCHED	8630	$1.25
☐	THE IMPETUOUS DUCHESS	8705	$1.25

Buy them at your local bookseller or use this handy coupon:

Barbara Cartland

The world's bestselling author of romantic fiction.
Her stories are always captivating tales of intrigue,
adventure and love.

☐	THE TEARS OF LOVE	2148	$1.25
☐	THE DEVIL IN LOVE	2149	$1.25
☐	THE ELUSIVE EARL	2436	$1.25
☐	THE BORED BRIDEGROOM	6381	$1.25
☐	JOURNEY TO PARADISE	6383	$1.25
☐	THE PENNILESS PEER	6387	$1.25
☐	NO DARKNESS FOR LOVE	6427	$1.25
☐	THE LITTLE ADVENTURE	6428	$1.25
☐	LESSONS IN LOVE	6431	$1.25
☐	THE DARING DECEPTION	6435	$1.25
☐	CASTLE OF FEAR	8103	$1.25
☐	THE GLITTERING LIGHTS	8104	$1.25
☐	A SWORD TO THE HEART	8105	$1.25
☐	THE MAGNIFICENT MARRIAGE	8166	$1.25
☐	THE RUTHLESS RAKE	8240	$1.25
☐	THE DANGEROUS DANDY	8280	$1.25
☐	THE WICKED MARQUIS	8467	$1.25
☐	LOVE IS INNOCENT	8505	$1.25
☐	THE FRIGHTENED BRIDE	8780	$1.25
☐	THE FLAME IS LOVE	8887	$1.25

Buy them at your local bookseller or use this handy coupon:

Bantam Book Catalog

It lists over a thousand money-saving best-sellers originally priced from $3.75 to $15.00 —bestsellers that are yours now for as little as 60¢ to $2.95!

The catalog gives you a great opportunity to build your own private library at huge savings!

So don't delay any longer—send us your name and address and 25¢ (to help defray postage and handling costs).